Down the length of the bar, the *estancieros* leaned back and away on either side as if a great wind had come blowing down the room.

"Get away!" McGee said, and struck at Lee's restraining arm as Nuñoz raised his revolver very quickly and aimed it at Lee all in a single movement, and smoothly.

Lee, McGee wrestling at his left side, drew and shot Gaspar Nuñoz—but didn't kill him. The bullet struck Nuñoz low on his left side, so that he was off balance as he fired. That round snapped barely past Lee's head as he pulled away from McGee and shot at Nuñoz again. Didn't see if he'd hit him.

Nuñoz lifted his revolver again, took the same deliberate aim.

Lee and Nuñoz fired together, the sounds of the gunshots unbearable in the room. Lee saw the lance of flame from Nuñoz's pistol, heard a loud smacking sound, and saw in the same instant Gaspar Nuñoz's head suddenly split like a struck melon.

A dead man—and Lee with not a wound on him.

"Mother of God," said Alphonso Gutierrez, "but you are quick with that pistol!"

Also in the *Buckskin* Series:

BUCKSKIN #12

RECOIL

ROY LEBEAU

LEISURE BOOKS NEW YORK CITY

A LEISURE BOOK®

March 2004

Published by

Dorchester Publishing Co., Inc.
200 Madison Avenue
New York, NY 10016

ISBN 0-8439-2355-5

Printed in the United States of America.

Visit us on the web at www.dorchesterpub.com.

BUCKSKIN #12

RECOIL

ONE

If anyone had asked Señor Rodriguez for a description of the *Yanqui* who had, the previous year, disembarked from the *Madre de Dios* at the *Riachuelo* docks, the Señor would have been able to provide it without hesitation.

Tall, and seeming young, with dark blond hair bleached somewhat lighter by the shipboard sun. Odd eyes—amber colored, like a rich woman's cat's. This fellow, this obvious *Yanqui* (and, as obviously, something of a ruffian) had limped deep off his left leg as he walked down the gangplank with a saddle and small bundle of possessions slung on his back. He had carried a whip as well, and a large revolver on his hip. Wore the sombrero of a Mexican.

A desperate man, Señor Rodriguez thought at the time. One of those rogues—a cattle or horse-herding rogue, this one, by the look of his high-heeled boots—one of thousands of such that had come through *La Boca* to infest the Argentine with their greed and violence. Worse than the Italians, some of them.

Had not this fellow chosen to accost him, to

speak with him, Señor Rodriguez (a dealer in tallow and hides, and, that very summer afternoon, attending the promised arrival of the *Stella Maris* from Valpariaso with a shipment of such) would still, no doubt, have remembered him. This limping fellow had a . . . presence. Something of that a *Capitan* of *gauchos* had that assured him notice even among the noisy crowds along the docks.

"Señor!"

The fellow had hailed Rodriguez in public in that fashion as if he were calling to a *negro,* rather than to a man of Spanish blood of the purest sort, a man of affairs and an old settler.

"Señor, may I speak with you?"

And all this in the coarsest sort of Mexican Spanish.

Still, to ignore him would be to give offense at the cost of dissatisfied curiosity—and perhaps something worse. This appeared a dangerous sort of a man. He possessed an *injured* look to the expression of his eyes. An odd expression . . .

Therefore, the *Stella Maris* being still apparently some great distance from Buenos Aires (only God in His superior wisdom knew where that Genoese priate was sailing with the tallow and hides) Señor Rodrigues discovered that there was time for a lunch with this importunate *Americano.* Coffee, *empanadas,* small cakes . . .

This person named himself Lee Morgan, then appeared to pause for a moment, sipping his coffee in the shadowed gloom under the cafe balcony's tin roof, his odd amber eyes resting on

Rodriguez's face as if their gaze itself had weight; pausing, perhaps, to see if Señor Rodriguez had recognized that name, even this far south. This fellow then, his name unrecognized and looking, across the small, rough-wood table, not as young as he had at a distance, demanded politely to be told of Argentina—all of it, and immediately.

He asked that courteously, in almost a gentlemanly way, and since he had insisted on paying for their meal though Rodriguez had protested, and on purchasing two bottles of Chilean wine as well, Rodriguez thought it a reasonable request.

The fellow wished to know of Buenos Aires, of course. He wished the glorious city described to him, from the Tango-bars along the waterfront, to the splendors of the *Plaza de Mayo*. And this, of course, it was Señor Rodriguez's great pleasure to do. Too few, in an ignorant world, knew of these splendors.

And then, of course, after the first bottle of wine, (it had to be admitted that the Chileans, though stupid and greedy where other nations' land might be concerned, had at least that single virtue of good wine-making) he wished to know of the *pampa*—the sea of grass.

The great *estancias,* their herds of cattle and horses . . . The cost of this grazing . . . The difficulty of water, and the windmills that overcame such difficulty. The endless extent of these *pampas* . . . and the temper of the men who held it . . . the temper of the men who worked it.

Señor Rodriguez, seduced by wine and his host's fathomless curiosity, found himself delivering to this undoubted fugitive a lecture on the perfections of the Argentine, its great size and wealth and beauty, a lesson and description of each particular Province, its grasslands or mountains or lakes, worthy of a *Maestro's* lecture at the University.

He also mentioned the Chaco, the Green Hell in the tropic northwest, that murderous swampland wilderness of jungle Indians, outlaws, disease and violence, where only fools or the desperate attempted to carve out new latter-day empires of beef or horseflesh.

He mentioned the Chaco so, passing.

Lee was riding perhaps three horse lengths behind the gaucho called Pico when that unfortunate took a Benudo arrow, a cloth-yard long and driven hard by a *chonta* palm bow, through the small of his back. The arrow had arrived from the yellow-green thorn brush walling the trail with a short high pitched snoring sound, then whacked into the gaucho's back, piercing him from left to right, transfixing both kidneys.

It was a killing blow, and the gaucho, after an instant's shocked silence, shrieked like a woman, arching in his saddle, reaching back with both hands to fumble at the barbed arrowhead protruding at his right side . . . the long ragged fletching sticking out at his left.

Pico arched back, and back further until Lee, the Bisley Colt's drawn and the dun booted left and into the wall of thorns, saw the man's anguished face, now upside down, his bent-brim hat touching his horse's crupper.

The dun went into the thorns, squealing as Lee kicked the long-shanked Spanish spurs in deep.

Lee bowed his head to let the weather-bleached sombrero take the sudden rake and puncture of the thorns—damned if he knew how the Benudos could creep through the stuff—and saw, just to the left, a short brown man in a colored shirt and no other clothes stepping neatly away through a yellow green haze of tangled thorn and guebracho branches, his great bow held in one hand like a spear.

Lee took a thorn deep in his right cheek. A brace of them lanced into his right leg as the dun turned under his spurs. Lee swung the Colt's across his saddle bow, leveled, and fired just as the small brown man stepped through a curtain of darker green and was gone.

Lee heard, in the crash of the shot, another sound—the quick thump of the bullet striking. He hauled the dun clear around by main force and drove his spurs in again. The horse bucketed and kicked, then barrelled on through green waterfalls of thorn into the darker green where the brown man had gone.

Lee saw the Indian's leg, and then the man, tumbled head first into the roots of the thicket, bare buttocks in the air. Lee saw no shit on them, assumed the fellow was still alive, and fired a second shot from the lunging dun into the fellow's ass.

The Benudo kicked at that, both legs kicking up

like a gigged frog, then stiffening like a woman being taken from behind. Trembling.

Lee pulled the dun up, felt thorns run into his hand on the reins, leaned down to the Indian, and fired again, into the man's back and broke his backbone.

The short, muscular brown legs relaxed at that, sprawled limp; a quick jet of brown liquid spurted into leaves.

"Did you get him?" McGee shouted out on the trail. *"You O.K. in there, Lee?"*

Sounded worried.

"O.K.!"

Lee swung down off the dun, cursing the animal as it shifted, stomping, amid the saber and stab of the thorns, and bent to see better what he had shot. Reached down with his left hand, and levered the corpse over.

Paused then, to look around him, as well as the thicket would allow. Wouldn't be caring to get what Pico had got just for not being careful.

No sign of another man. And the dun was quieting.

This dead one was a Benudo, no doubt about those blue bands of tattooing—two wide bands across each cheek. The man's nostrils were pierced for quill ornaments, though like most of these savages, he was likely in some sort of mourning, and so went about with an undecorated nose.

Older man. Perhaps thirty. Quite old for a forest Indian, though Lee understood that the pampa tribes, the plains Indians to the south, lived longer as a rule, or had done so before General

Roca's cavalry began cutting them short.

This man's eyes were open, but they didn't make him look alive. The open eyes were the color of black coffee with dust blown over it.

Shame to do a man that way, plug him in the ass like a sissy. But the damn thorn had left no choice about it.

Lee reached into his right boot, slid free his double-edge dagger, shorter in the blade than the slender gaucho knives, reached behind the Indian's head for his cropped top-knot (not enough there, really, for a good grip) and, with an easy circular motion of his wrist, carved out a circle in the man's hair (the dagger-tip grating on bone)—then tugged once, then again, and freed a small black-thatched clump of scalp. Snapped it like a snot-rag to pop the blood off it, then tucked it into his gunbelt.

The gauchos would like to see some sign of vengeance. Would, likely, want to bury the scalp with Pico when he went, as he certainly would. That arrow shot had been a killing shot, for sure.

"Poor man," McGee said, speaking Spanish to Lee without thinking of it, just as Lee did with him. Lee felt at times that he had lost his English entirely, having spoken and often thought in Spanish now for something over two years. He could have spoken English with McGee, of course, who'd been born foreign like so many Argentines (Irish from County Antrim, in McGee's case) but for whatever reason, they did not do so.

With Englishmen, of course, there was no choice. These beef-buyers, businessmen, agents and investors would not usually stoop to speaking Spanish, and certainly not with scrub ranchers, Irish-born, Yankee-born or whatever.

"Poor man," McGee said, bending over the gaucho like a mother. McGee, in his forties, blocky, weather-tanned, his hair already grizzled grey, had a rough way with men, usually—Lee had seen him beat a *mestizo,* a man from Paraguay, nearly to death with a cane-bottom chair in Revadavia, the *mestizo* having offered to cheat the Irishman over a sale of baled alfalfa. But with injured animals or men, the Irishman was gentle as a woman. Something to do with his own hard times earlier, Lee supposed. McGee was easy with his daughter, too; always saw that Sarita had some Indian woman to do the heavy work, laundry and such, about his place.

"Poor man . . ."

Pico lay in the middle of the trail, two of the gauchos kneeling beside him, holding his hands. The other two, Lee's men—a very tall, toothless wrangler named Arturo and a shorter man, dirty, fat, his baggy gaucho trousers tied up over the bulge of a considerable belly—stood guard up and down the trail with Winchester .44's, gifts that Lee had made to all his men at considerable expense. The fat gaucho was named Nacio Fortún, and had had some reputation as a man of violence even among the gauchos (not a peaceable group, taken as a whole). He had bridled, early in his employment, when Lee had told him to muck the stock stalls a second day running. The fat man had muttered something, turned a slow murderous look on Lee with eyes as dark, round, and dull as a piranha's.

Had stood stone still in the yard and tossed the spade at Lee's feet. And waited to see if Lee intended to do anything about it.

Nacio Fortún, like many gauchos, carried a small revolver tucked into the back of his wide belt. This was a useful piece against snakes or sun-mad wild cows, and was also used by these men though inexpertly, when cantina quarrels escalated beyond sensible settlement with knives. Gauchos almost never fought with their fists— they thought it undignified— though Lee had seen men kicked to death a time or two. So, with Nacio Fortún, it would have to be knife, or revolver, or turn away from the fat man and let him be.

Lee couldn't let it pass. No 'Patron' could ever let such behavior pass. It would ruin him; it would cost him his land. There were hundreds of land-hungry drifters in the Chaco and among those, perhaps twenty or thirty truly dangerous men, clever men, who would be very interested to hear that the *Yanqui* who had bought twenty thousand acres from Juan McGee had not the heart to govern his gauchos—and likely not to hold that twenty thousand acres, either.

This could not, therefore, be allowed to pass.

"There are three things that you can do," Lee had said to the fat man. "You can get your horse and ride off this place. Or you can pick up that spade and start shoveling shit. Or you can take out your knife, and then we will see if there are any balls hiding under that belly.''

Nacio Fortún had chosen the third, and Lee had had no choice but to draw his boot-knife to fight the man. No gaucho had any chance in a pistol fight against an American gunman and the men knew it. Rifles were their real weapons, and they were very good with them. Rifles . . . and knives.

This same Nacio, only a stub left of his right ear, now stood guard down the trail. Changed in no way from the rough he had been, save that he was now pleased to follow Lee where he was told to. Grumbled, but shoveled manure when he was told to as well.

A good man made by a knife-cut.

And if Lee had strolled back to the head-quarters hut afterward with his hands in his pockets to hide their shaking, that was something the gauchos had no need to know. The fat man had been very quick with his slender, foot-long blade. Very quick . . .

McGee and one of his men tried to lift Pico up gently. The stricken man then made a dreadful face, and drew a sudden heaving, whistling breath. The scream was already in his throat when they laid him back down in the dirt.

"Jesus, Mary, and Joseph . . ." McGee looked up at Lee. Lee had noticed that since McGee's wife had died, the Irishman looked to him as he hadn't when Lee first came into the country riding the Tucuman train, lame as a kicked dog, and carrying almost thirty thousand stolen Mexican pesos. Then, McGee had been the teacher, the 'Patron,' and had only grudgingly sold Lee the twenty thousand acres of raw Chaco . . . the *Impenetrable,* it was called. Dry swamp and wet graze. Scrub, thorn, and some of the damnedest greenest jungle Lee had ever dreamed of.

Indians, too, the Benudos and others. Benudos the only real bad ones, and they as bad as any Lee had heard of. Deep forest Indians come down to the south to raid for beef and dogs . . . come down to the south for the pure mischief of it, Lee thought.

McGee and the gauchos were looking up at Lee as if he might be God Almighty—as if he might reach down and yank the long arrow from Pico's back, touch the two wounds and heal them.

"Get out of the way," Lee said.

Stared up at him, Pico, too, the little gaucho's eyes agonized as a dying child's.

"Get out of my way," Lee said, lifted the coils of the black-snake whip off his left shoulder, hefted the long lead-weighted handle in his left hand—and as McGee and the gaucho ducked out of his way, took a long striding step, the whip handle high and brought it whistling down across the side of Pico Vasquez' head.

Made a sound like a dropped board.

"Oh, damnit, man! You've killed him!"

And might have. Pico lay flat out, his legs trembling, eyes turned up into his head. Lee thought he might have felt something give under the swing of the whip handle. Perhaps something had cracked there.

"So much the better if I have killed him," Lee said. "Unless you want to be carrying him across a horse, yelling all the way to Resistencia. Let that butcher-doctor there play him with his instruments for a while before he dies."

Neither McGee nor his gauchos had anything to say to that. Nor to the possible Benudos that Pico's screams might have brought from the scrub.

"You put him back on his horse now," Lee said, "and lead him on out. Sooner we're gone from here, the better." The Benudos sometimes came out one by one—older men trying to prove they retained their magic, boys trying to prove they'd achieved it. Sometimes one by one.

Usually not.

"Put him up, Juan."

McGee nodded, weary as a washerwoman, got to his feet and gestured to his men.

Pico made a small bundle over his saddle, lashed firm but not so tight as to hurt him. McGee's gauchos, sentimental, were weeping as they finished the ties.

Sentimental . . . violent. So like his men had been in Idaho. For an instant, Lee felt quite ill with homesickness. The smell of heat and blood and horses and horse-leather. Enough to make him sick.

They rode out of the *quebracho* scrub a few hours later, into a late afternoon sun.

They rode then to the Rio Dulce, where its mild riffling rapids stirred among the stones. They were then forty miles upstream from Santiago del Estero. When they reached the Dulce, as if he had been waiting for that, Pico Vasquez farted and died. A gaucho—Columbo, one of McGee's men —rode up alongside of Pico's horse, reached down to lift the man's head where he draped across the saddle, bound, and found Pico indeed dead. Dead as mutton.

They pulled up then, untied the little man, took him down, dug out a shallow trench with their knives, put Pico into it (Lee stooping to press his eyes closed) then filled the place and set rocks from the river over the loose dirt.

If any of the gauchos thought that Lee might have struck too hard with the whip handle, they didn't blame him for it. To the contrary.

McGee prayed over the grave for a short while. The Irishman was more a son of the Church than the Argentine and Paraguayan gauchos. These men had too much Indian in them to be perfectly comfortable with Holy Mother Church. Wasn't one of them didn't have owl bones or puma shit or a dry and withered scrap of afterbirth in a small leather bag at their throats.

Hadn't done Pico Vasquez any good, of course.

After closing Pico's eyes, Lee had taken the Benudo's blood-caked scalp out of his belt, muttered something over it, drew it across the dead man's forehead three times, then tossed it onto the corpse's chest before the grave was filled over.

The gauchos had watched this with some interest and satisfaction, and Lee had been satisfied himself to add to his very slight and local stature as an *hungano* with access to certain minor *loas* and cattle spirits. A medicine man. "A damned mountebank," according to McGee.

The thorn wounds were stinging something fierce. Lucky he hadn't lost an eye riding into that thicket. The dun had an easy gait, was a good horse for Chaco stock. Pleased enough, now it had had its drink from the Dulce.

Lee heard the gauchos murmuring behind him on the trail, one of them singing "Santa Rosita " as he rode. Likely Arturo, toothless man made for strange singing. But damned if that man couldn't eat the toughest meat cooked just by gumming the stuff to strings. And no meat tougher than scrub northwestern beef. Made a man want to weep for old McCorkle. *There* was a cook could have tamed even Chaco beef. Would have made a ragout of it to cheer.

McGee was silent, riding beside him.

The Irishman was becoming a concern. Lee thought about McGee as he rode along, scanning the brush on their side of the river. Not likely the Indios would be scouting this open country. Not too likely.

Conchata McGee had ridden out one afternoon to find a Spanish-bred colt named Torio that had jumped their corral and bolted, apparently for lack of anything else to do.

That had been in January, the deepest of the season's heat in this below-the-equator backwards weather. It had been a Tuesday, and the thermometer at Galvez Feed had shown 109 degrees Fahrenheit, something less Celcius.

Conchata had been a heavy woman, solid built and tough as whang leather. Old Spanish stock, and not a touch of the red in her. A slight mustache . . . heavy breasts. Eyes as beautiful as a deer's. That Tuesday, she rode out on a horse named Pinto—though it was a solid black—and got as far as the bañados down by the river, when the horse bucked her off. Lee had always thought it was a snake scared the black, since Conchata McGee was not the sort of woman who fell off her horse as a regular thing. Lee thought it was probably a snake, since the reptiles loved those wet places where the swamp water lay only an inch or so deep in the high grass, so that the winter sun, the fiercest Lee had ever known, heated it too hot for a man to drink.

Whatever its cause for spooking, the black had thrown her, and thrown her hard enough so that her right leg was broken at the thigh bone when she fell, the end of the bone pushing out clear through the muscle and white skin.

She had a pistol in her belt, one of the trashy little French revolvers the gauchos fancied, and appeared to have fired several shots, hoping for help. It was an understandable thing to have done, though it put her in some jeopardy from Indians.

No help in any case. The nearest men to her were probably Alphonso's and those would have been eight or nine miles down the Paraña, at the tannery. So no one heard those shots.

It appeared, according to Lunapé, who tracked

for the *estancieros* from time to time (when he wasn't too drunk), that the lady had lain injured so severely and quite still for perhaps a half of an hour before she began to crawl . . . crawling with the most wonderful slowness to try and catch up that black horse which ever and always, as is a horse's nature, moved just the smallest bit further away as she came closer. Crawling through hot water puddles and high grass, crawling in a cloud of stinging midges, of black flies buzzing, clustering at the fresh blood on her riding skirts, where the big bone had come tearing through.

McGee had ridden home, by luck, that afternoon—not due, really, for another day and more—found her missing and no note left for him, and had ridden belly to ground to whip Lunapé off his fat squaw and on the trace.

One of McGee's gauchos riding a five-mile cast ahead of Lunapé loping found Conchata McGee at sunset. Found her by the kites circling.

The broken leg, it proved, had not destroyed her.

It was the sun.

This sturdy, clever, fierce Spanish woman who, with McGee, had made a pair which no men took lightly in this cruelest of all countries. This lovely-eyed white-skinned woman, as proud of her sun-protected paleness (hard won in the Chaco) as any society queen in Buenos Aires, had lost her sombrero in her fall.

Had crawled her dreadful crawl bare-headed but for the black and glossy braids—almost perfectly black, with only here and there the faintest drift of ash grey—of her thick hair. Had crawled bare-headed under the Chaco sun in midwinter, shaded only by the clouds of flies that swarmed her . . . the occasional fleeting shadow of a kite, swinging high overhead.

The sun had slowly, over the course of slow hours, baked her brains in the vessel of her skull.

When Eusébio found her, this lady lay sprawled, her skirts thrown high as if she'd been raped, to show red-soaked thighs, the wrist-thick blue-white end of bone thrust out near her groin. Her eyes were half closed, only the whites showing. Her tongue, swollen and purple as a man's cock, had forced her mouth wide open. Quite unconscious, she was grunting softly, as if she were in intercourse or was moving her bowels.

Eusébio swung down, bent to gently draw her skirt down over her spraddled legs, her injury, then soaked his bandanna from his canteen—not wanting to use the hot and bloody water where she lay—and used that wet cloth to cover her head. The heat of her head came through the cloth like a stove's heat. Under that cloth, he delicately dripped the slighest thread of water along her lips, over the purple knot of her tongue.

That was how they were when Lunapé came trotting. McGee and another man riding just behind.

One sort of McGee rode to that spot.

A different man of the same name climbed off his horse, calling his wife's name.

And a third man—different again, though still named McGee—took her home.

It was this third man, this third McGee, that Lee now rode beside. Occasionallly, there were echoes in him of what he had been, but only occasionally. Grief had come down on him like sudden weather and worn him away.

Conchata McGee had lived for two months, with McGee and Sarita beside her bed both day and night. They had bought ice—or had tried to buy it; Lazlo had made them a gift of all they could freight out of his ice house up on the Alto. They had brought this ice down from the mountains packed in sawdust and hay bales. It was a week's hard teamstering cross-country, with most of the ice melting and running down through the wagon floorboards to splash along the trail dust and vanish in the heat. But some remained after each trip, enough to pack around her as she lay grunting in her soaked bed, her broken leg set by Karl Klinger, who was a fair hand at doctoring animals.

She was quite blind, though she stared at McGee and his daughter as if she could see them. She was not deaf, though. If they spoke to her long enough, in loud enough voices, she would sometimes sit half up and stop her grunting, and seem to listen. Occasionally—once, when Lee was there—she would lie quiet for a while, then suddenly rouse and make a loud explosive sound.

A sound like "*Blawww . . .!*" Very loud.

There was nothing human in that sound.

When she died, and for a while after that, Lee

had watched to see if McGee would recover. Now, though, he knew the man would not. Some men, it seemed to Lee, could gather courage throughout their lives, lose it over this or that, then gather it again. He thought himself to be one of those sort of men.

Others, though, seemed born with a stock of bravery, sometimes a great stock of courage, more than enough to last out their lives. But these men had no way to gather more.

McGee was spent. There was no more heart left in him—not for hard roads. In Buenos Aires, even in Salta or Resistencia, he might live out an honored life in some sort of tanning business or lumber business, or alfalfa feed.

Not out on the Chaco.

He was no longer strong enough for it.

Sarita, of course, still had her courage. It is easy to be brave at seventeen. But she would not last. Soon enough, there would be an accident on the *estancia,* or sickness in the herds, or trouble with a drunken gaucho. Then she would see her father bend. Bend, and then break.

No girl could hold a rancho out here. Men would come riding from Paraguay, or local men would come riding, or one of her father's men. One or more of them would come for her some night when the moon hung over the cordillera of the Andes like a great ball of cracked crystal. The men, or man alone, would break into the house, beat McGee, and take her. Then, if he were strong enough, he would take the *estancia* and hold it and all its lands.

The cavalry out of Resistencia stayed clear of such personal troubles. It was, Lee thought, a policy of letting the violent settle violent country without too much interference from Buenos Aires.

All this meant trouble for Lee. Trouble for the Stirrup. His twenty thousand acres marched alongside McGee's for seven miles up the Paraña. He'd bought his land from McGee—land too rough, too wet in some places, too dry in others. McGee had been just willing to part with it, for silver pesos.

But now McGee was weakening; his Iron Hoof would, in a few months, a year or so at most, become the prey of other, stronger men.

And the man who took Iron Hoof's forty thousand acres would have a strangling hold on Lee's ranch.

Something to think about. And something else to think about with it: it might be Lee who proved the strong man come to take Sarita and her father's land. Lee had no doubt that he could kill McGee—likely could have killed him when the Irishman was in his prime. Could certainly kill him now. Openly . . . or in ambush. Easy enough to blame the Benudos, to say that *Cuchillo* himself had come out of the *Mato* to raid.

And what then?

Then it would be *Don* Lee throughout the Chaco. That Don would own sixty thousand acres of grazing and lumber and cotton.

That Don would also have Sarita McGee— short, strong, neat-bodied, her hair as black, her skin as pale as her mother's had been. Her eyes were her father's, a dark China blue. Not really a beautiful girl. Nose too big, mouth too wide. Could do with more of a length of leg on her . . .

But he'd have her. Wear her down. Get rid of that quick, jeering temper of hers, those Hidalgo airs she so enjoyed—as if she were not a half-breed *Chacana,* truth to tell.

He'd have her then, if he had to beat her down to size.

Lee knew of only two men who might try to block him at all this. Gaspar Nuñoz, for certain. Philipe Orellana as well. Might be others come around. Drifters, Paraguayans. Nothing, he thought, that could not be handled.

Capitan Cortés would stand clear. The cavalry-man too much of Buenos Aires and the *pampa* to want to brawl for a half-Irish girl and a few thousand acres of wilderness. Cortés' people owned their own land.

The tasks therefore would be to kill McGee, to take the girl and the estancia, and then to kill Nuñoz when Nuñoz came to kill him. Orellana might stay clear of it after all. He loved Sarita, but he might stay clear if Lee'd already taken her. A fastidious man, Orellana. The Argentines didn't care for cream-leavings.

And what then—this all accomplished?

An oven bird cried its clattering call and bustled away through the air above them, sooty black, quick flashes of dark green as it flew. McGee rode beside Lee in silence, the curled, narrow brim of his flat-topped sombrero shading his face in deep shadow. Lee couldn't see his eyes.

Well, what then? That all tried and accomplished . . . Get the land, the crops—then sell them? Go back north—back to the States?

Buy back Spade Bit? Try to get the old crew together?

Likely not.

Not back to Spade Bit. And the crew . . . the crew was likely dead, now, one or two of them. The others drifted . . . successful, unsuccessful. Bud Bent . . . Charlie Potts . . . Ford, and Sefton. McCorkle might be dead by now, or cooking in some fancy hotel in Boise.

No. Not back to Spade Bit.

Spade Bit was safe, deep in the arms of the past. No use to try and bring it back. Wouldn't be the same . . . couldn't be the same, in any case.

Is Buckskin Frank Leslie's boy grown up at last?

Perhaps.

Grown up enough to contemplate the cold murder of a friend. That was fairly grown up, for sure.

They turned from the river now, riding west out across an ever-stretching flat, the few dwarf quebrachos throwing evening shadows. The grass muffled the strike of their horses' hooves. A long ride after Indians (the occasion some half dozen of hamstrung cattle, a *mestizo* woman old enough to be a great-granny staked out, blinded, then disemboweled). A long ride—and one shot Indian, one skewered gaucho the result of it.

Evenings after rides like this, two-day rides with little rest, Lee thanked God and common sense that he had kept his saddle out of Mexico and across Argentina to this country.

The Brazos double-rig felt the only friend his hind parts had; the gaucho saddles were fierce enough to ruin a civilized man. Bad as McClellans, though almost as easy on the horses.

So, thank God for his saddle which now felt only like a cactus bed rather than a bed of coals.

Lee had come into this country on the Tucuman train out of Buenos Aires after a long lunch talk with a fat man on the *Plato* docks, and a longer week in the tango palaces of La Boca. Hard to say whether he had danced more than he fucked, or the other way 'round. Had certainly had a caution of a time with two sisters—one twelve, the other fourteen—who had introduced more variety in bed-play than a reasonable man might have imagined possible. Had grown to appreciate that waterfront in just those few days and had had only one fight (to the death, regrettably) with a pimp named Sabastién Sarmiento.

Boca days . . .

Then the train to Tucuman, still, surprisingly, with most of the Mexican pesos in his possibles. Later, on reflection, he had realized how unlikely that had been. The long, slow ride on an Argentine cattle train, figuring to see the *Chaco,* just in case—drawn to it as, apparently, the roughest, newest part of the country, and so, probably less nicely policed—less nice in every particular. Would try that country first. Then, if he dared, turn south and east for the great *pampa,* the sea of grass that never found a shore.

Cattle country. Perfect horse country.

A man might find wealth there, might found a dynasty, if he had the courage (and the luck) to do it. Might become one of the great *estancieros*, one of the men that ruled the country.

Possible down there.

Not in the *Gran Chaco*. In the Chaco a man might become rich. Might, in truth, become a great man. But he would never rule the country. In the Chaco, nature ruled, not man.

So Lee had proposed to himself a visit to this rougher section—a sort of settling down into the Argentine wilderness, perhaps for months, perhaps for a year or two. Then down to the real horse country, where fine animals might be raised, the equal of any on earth, and raised healthy, not ridden with worms and blow-flies, not snake-bitten, or hammered by the heat.

Down to the real horse country, and in a few months. Or so he thought on the Tucuman train to Sante Fe. So he thought until the morning of the eighth day of the train ride (not liking railroad trains any more than he ever had). On the morning of that day, the cattle train had rattled slowly across the Chaco. Rolling slowly across desert and swamp alternately, endless, blazing with the most desperate heat. Lee had swung out and climbed up the ladder to the railcar roof, hoping for some slight breath of air made by the train's slow passage.

He had found no cooler air, only the baking heat-shriveled roof planks, their red paint long ago scrubbed off by heat and light and torrential rain.

Planks too hot to sit on.

Lee had stood, balancing easily to the slow rocking, the clunk-a-clunk of the wheels along narrow, rusting rails—had looked up ahead, up past the small bell-funneled engine, its nasty puffs of greasy smoke. Had looked up higher—and seen the Andes.

Those distant, very distant mountains, black and white, cool and towering, jagged peak after peak standing off to the west, to Chile and the sea.

Like the Rockies.

Like home.

TWO

At full dark, they came to the headquarters of the
Stirrup, the brand burned deep into a shave-sided
quebracho log driven down into the red Chaco
dirt. They'd been riding Lee's land already for
more than two hours. Lee asked the others in for
rum, or yerba maté, or rice and beans, but McGee
was worried about Sarita . . . must continue on to
his home. Even so, Lee called for maté and sticks
of sugar cane, and bony Bonifacia came running,
skinny nigger legs invisible in the gloom, seeming
to float in her pale flour sack dress as she brought
the tea gourds and sugar cane to the mounted
men.

McGee and his gauchos sat their weary mounts,
each man sucking at the hot herb tea through his
own silver straw. Then McGee and his man
Eusébio each took a glass of rum.

"Bad luck," McGee said to Lee, leaning down
to hand his glass back to Bonifacia. "Bad luck."

The moon was just rising over the mountains to
the west. A man looking that way might have seen
the silver of snow across the highest peaks
reflecting faintly in the moonlight. But on the

Stirrup, the night heat lay like an oven's breath. Fireflies swarmed flickering through the chupa and flowering peach that grew rough hedges along the Stirrup's huts and stables.

One of these insects crawled on Juan McGee's hand where it rested on his saddle-bow, and there pulsed out its slow small periods of yellow light.

"Foolish to go after them," McGee said, and Lee saw the mounted gauchos listening. "Wasn't worth losing Pico for."

Worse and worse.

"Juan—ride on home now, or stay over here."

McGee brushed the firefly away. "One of the best men I had . . ."

"God damnit, Juan, the man took his chances the same as the rest of us! What was done, had to be done! Now, you ride home, and get some sleep."

McGee sighed a weary sigh, nodded, and turned his horse's head. He led his men out of the Stirrup yard at a walk, the tired horses hanging their heads, the gauchos sagging in their saddles. It had been a long ride, with death at the end of it. Fights, even little fights like that one, coursing back and forth through the thorn thickets, hunting the Benudos, tended to weary men. Fear of dying wore them out, Lee supposed. He'd been worn that way more than once himself.

He stood beside the wild grape arbor, watching the last of McGee's men ride out of the moonlight into the scrub shadows down alongside the run that drained the estancia. Run un-named, as far as Lee knew. He hadn't cared to name it, himself.

Lee stood for a few moments looking out into the night. Odd, how close the jungle seemed in the night. Was several miles away, actually, over the Paraña. In the daylight, a man hardly thought about it except for seeing the occasional agouti, or capybara. Sometimes a fér-de-lance or anaconda down in the marshlands and bañados. But in the night, the jungle seemed to move across the river, grow closer to the ranch lands as if the trees, once the sun was down, commenced to walk. The heat of it, the smells . . . bird calls, too. All seemed closer by night.

The Green Hell, these people called it—and so it was for any poor devil that stepped more than a few yards into it. Only a few yards, and if a man had no friend to shout him out, he might wander deeper and deeper, circling slow mile-wide circles (thinking he was walking straight as a string) walking through silence broken only by distant bird calls, distant troops of monkeys shouting through the tree tops two hundred feet up. Walking through suffocating heat . . . all in a permanent twilight, shadows too deep for a man to see a bird-spider until the plate-sized thing scrambled out from under his feet. Walking . . . then crawling . . .

Not for the Indians, of course. To them, Lee supposed, the *Mato* was not terrible, was rather something of a great palace, green, and gloomy, stretching welcoming on to their villages and then beyond, a thousand miles and more into the great bason of the Amazon.

Whichever—by night, it seemed to move.

And there, tonight, deep into it—perhaps two miles, perhaps ten—a Benudo village would be in mourning, the men's faces painted solid black now, the women wailing and slicing the flesh of their arms with saw grass knives or blades of trade iron. They would know of the death of the Benudo Lee killed, would have known of it within a few hours.

And at that village, or another, the old headman called by the whites and mestizos *El Cuchillo* would be considering a response.

Lee turned and walked back across the yard toward the house. Place looked mighty mean still —a raw new *estancia* among other older Chaco ranches, none of which was any sort of a show-place. None of them the great prairie mansions of the pampas.

Tin-roofed house of adobe brick—more a shack than a house, at that, and tin-roofed rather than palm-thatched because Lee had preferred to spend the cash on that than worry about fire arrows coming in and a bunch of Indians following— though, in truth, that wasn't the forest savages' style.

That mean shack, a walk-way kitchen, and, in back, the lean-to sheds the gauchos lived in with their women. These gauchos too ignorant, wild, and horny for the bunk-house life. Too ignorant, wild, and horny to be good for anything, really, except droving.

They fitted the cattle well enough. A sorrier lot of fly-blown scrubs Lee had never seen. He'd had four big corrals built on Stirrup, two here at headquarters, the other two out on the flats to the west. Used those two as holding pens—one for sick stock, the other for those animals that showed some promise of breeding to meat rather than bone and horn.

McGee, Alphonso Suarez, Karl Klinger, Gaspar Nuñoz and the others had had some fun over Lee's breeding plans, Nuñoz in his finely handsome Hidalgo style, the others more bluntly.

"Keep zem fuckin' t'ings *alive!*" Karl Klinger at the Kit Kat Club in Sante Fe, in the course of finishing his fifth rum sour. "Keep 'dese fuckin' beefs alive—zen you talk of breeding!"

He was right, of course. Wrong, too. True, you could not breed dead cattle for quality meat. But neither could you ever get quality animals without careful breeding. And that included breeding the stayers, the bulls and cows that *didn't* go down in the heat, that *didn't* develop blow-fly sores a man could put his fist into.

The Chaco was not Idaho and never could be. There wasn't the winter to kill off the flies, the worms. On the other hand, neither was Idaho the Chaco. No *estanciero* had ever lost a herd to blizzard or starvation either. Not in a country where even a careless farmer could grow two crops of cotton (for cloth and cotton-seed) or two crops of alfalfa in a season, and even two crops of corn, if the land would stand it.

Of course, if a man needed a doctor to be within call—say, within two or three hundred miles—or if a man couldn't bear one-hundred-and-fifteen-degree heat for the winter months, or if a man was disturbed by large insects, and very many of them, or if a man didn't care to deal with *Mestizo* gauchos and bandits and cavalry deserters (usually all in the same persons) who would as cheerfully spit in your eye as carve your guts out . . . Well, if a man was as touchy as that, if he was that particularly nice, there was likely no pleasure for him to find in the stock business in the Argentine *Chaco*.

A man of that sort who had, say, stolen some thirty-odd thousand of Mexican pesos after a small scrap in the mountains of the pleasant country, would be advised to repair at once to Paris, France, and spend it.

A fellow, now, who had not been quite that sensible could find himself on a shocking piece of land in murderous country, with a ranch built of mud, tin, thorn brush, scrub cattle, grim rum and grimmer eats, with fence wire that rusted to flakes after three months of posts, and a collection of brown men as cow pokers who used bolas and tail-throws rather than honest rope, who could not hit a barn from the inside with a revolver, and who enjoyed few things as much as desperate duels with long-bladed knives.

And was all this enjoyable?

Lee supposed that it was. For it appeared to him as natural as breathing. The damned Chaco seemed to suit him right to the ground. If it weren't for the worry about McGee . . . Sarita. Riding for hard falls, both of them.

He stomped up the three plank steps to the porch, trying to shed some of the red mud so that

Bonifacia would not be spending the next day on all fours, scrubbing and moaning at once about the pain in her knees. Gaucho sombreros were nothing much, and gaucho saddles were worse, but the soft-top boots were prime for comfort. A man could even walk in them if he wanted to.

"Señor?"

"Not liable to be anybody else," Lee said. The old black woman, one of the few coloreds Lee had seen in this country, had been a servant at a colonel's house in Sante Fe before she was turned out for stealing. She'd told Lee that directly when she'd begged some small change from him outside the stockyard at Tucuman, then asked if he had a woman to keep his house. "But not the bed, Señor," she'd said. "I'm too old for it." She'd made a poking gesture, her forefinger through other forefinger and thumb, circled. "Also, white men are very bad at it." She'd not been a great temptation herself, being at least sixty—or looking it—and having only one eye, the left. A wrinkled black lid drooped over an empty socket on the right.

Since then, Bonifacia had proved herself an heroic floor polisher, the floor being *quebracho* puncheon, and not liable to shine high no matter what. Had proved herself there, and as a bulk cooker of tough meat to tougher steak, rice, beans, corn, corn cakes, and several varieties of sausages, all tasting alike, all difficult to chew, more difficult to swallow.

She had stolen nothing from him, since Lee kept nothing to steal except some blankets, his guns, hose tack, tally book, and a shelf of canned corned beef, peaches, tomatoes, pickles, and anchovy fish from Chile. Bonifacia was trustworthy with any property but jewelry. Jewelry of any sort, even the cheapest, was catnip to her.

Lee had a stem-winding watch, and it had a silver case, but old woman apparently regarded it as a tool, not decoration, for she left it alone.

The old woman drifted, nearly invisible in the darkness, before him into the house. She never lit lamps when Lee was out at night.

Lee scratched a Lucifer on his boot sole, lit a coal oil lantern at the table.

Her only eye, rheumy and yellow as a menagerie lion's, observed him by lamplight. "You killed only one of the animals?"

"One."

"And that fool Pico is no more?"

"No more."

Bonifacia hawked and spat—she did that often in disapproval—and since she would not dirty her floor, she always spat neatly down into her right hand, saving the spittle to scrub off at the kitchen bucket later.

"In my day," she sakd, "there were gauchos who *were* gaucho! Toledano! Chucho de Leon! They would have devoured the women in trousers who ride for this place!" The yellow eye considered. "Possibly you as well . . ."

"That mighty?" Lee said, sat, and held out a leg so she could wrestle the boot off. "Dangerous as that, were they?"

Bonifacia wrenched the boot off as if it were a

yard-hen's head. "Wonderfully dangerous men," she said. "Toledano would as soon gut a man as a fish, and as neatly." She reached down for the other boot, hauled it free. "You have not seen men of that sort," she said, "and now, it is too late. Now, there are only capons . . ."

"Oh, I've seen men of that sort," Lee said. "Those who weren't mad—were sad."

Bonifacia spat down into her cupped left hand; it was rare to have a two-spit conversation with her. "Happiness," she said, "is not the business of men."

"Pull up your skirt," Lee said, "and show me paradise, or go and get my dinner."

Bonifacia grunted in some disgust and faded away out of the lamplight, spittle clenched in both fists. Lee drew his tally book to him, flipping through the sweat stained pages, reading down the smudged columns by wavering lamplight.

Two thousand four hundred and seventy-nine beeves.

Not what might be called a grand herd, not even for the Chaco. Not negligible, however. Not negligible. And the stock some of the best beef in Northern Argentina. Red ribbon stock at the Sante Fe show at Christmas. Only Philipe Orellana had done as well from this part of the country. No prize for the bull, though. Damned animal was too small for best breeding. Lee had read that look on the judge's face, a damned Italian from the Capital—Rizzo, or something of that sort. Had put his stick on Diablo's shoulder, raised his eyebrows . . .

Lee would like to have a peso-tenth for every day that some fat white Italian bull would last on the Stirrup. The cows would likely kill him before the heat could. Fuck him to death . . .

Bonifacia came floating out of the dark with a tin coffee mug and a tin plate, set them both down beside the book.

Rice and beans and chunks of meat. Capybara, probably, soaked in cottonseed oil and chilis. Smelled worse than it tasted, thanks to the chilis. The coffee would be good—Lee bought Brazilian best for Stirrup; safe enough doing it, since the gauchos preferred maté.

He started to eat, noticing Bonifacia drifting out of the kitchen walkway again, hovering near the side door to watch him. For some female reason or other, she appeared to enjoy watching him eat. Behind her, voices of other women in the kitchen shed, getting dinners out of the two big pots for their own men. A thing Lee had introduced—one big meal each day, cooked in the main kitchen by Bonifacia. It left gauchos' women with some freedom for their babies . . . the small, pot-bellied brown children that infested the *estancia,* scurrying here and there, shouting, pissing wherever they happened to stand, dragging pet ocelot cubs, pet agouties, pet dogs, pet *caimans* along behind them, each tied by a length of baling twine to his small master, lover, and torturer.

This business of children on a place and in such numbers was a novel matter to Lee. In the States, it was only a very senior drover who might earn a cabin to himself fit to keep a woman in. Not so with these gauchos of the Chaco, whatever might be the proper in the pampas. These men needed their wives with them in the night. ("Wives" by courtesy.) Needed someone to brag to, as much as the necessary screwing, Lee supposed. And, in their turn, the women (bar an occasional quarrel, beating, or knifing) helped somewhat to civilize men whose mothers or grandfathers, more often than not, had worn toucan feathers, and shell ornaments through their noses.

These swarms of children, at first an annoyance, had become a pleasure to Lee. He had come to enjoy their noise, their constant little tragedies and triumphs. Not always such little tragedies, either. Four of the children had died in the last year, two of some sort of disease, two others otherwise. A caiman had taken one of them —a boy named Manuel Rivas, just seven years old, down at the Paraña. The mother, a fat woman named Isabelita, had gone mad when she saw it. The creature had bitten away the child's lower half, left the rest.

The second child, also a boy, had been attacked by stray dogs and killed.

It was capybara for sure—had that rank, oily taste to it. Lee kept eating, glad enough to have even such messes in his belly. Had been a damn long ride, with nothing but corn cake and iron beef jerky, canteen-hot maté . . .

Tomorrow first thing, have to go out to the flats near Margenita, bring in the calves. It would be a nice chore, chousing those strays out of that piece of rough. Take them a day, even if he took four, five men with him. It would leave Hernán and José to work fence by the river; they could carpenter the house corral afterward. That damn stud Sportivo had kicked two rails out of the south side . . .

And the feed. He'd have to go in to Resistencia before the end of the week, pay Alvarez with the yearling money. It would leave him short once the men were paid, but not too short, thanks to the cotton. Thanks to the lumbering, too. A fool's game, to be sending his logs down the Paraña to those mills. Build his own mill—that would be the sensible thing to do. Borrow the money in Sante Fe, if he didn't mind putting up the *estancia,* lock, stock and barrel. Might be cleverer to go in with Orellana. He'd be talking about a mill further down the river, but not too far for Lee's timber.

It would mean shares with Orellana—going fifty-fifty. Orellana, of course, was a gentleman, would be good as his word in any agreement. He also, of course, would insist on fair dealing with all the mill customers. First come, first served would be the rule for sawing and stripping and finishing.

Orellana's honor could cost a partner money.

It bore thinking of . . .

"Patron . . ."

"Yes?" Bonifacia came into the light.

"You wish Corazon?"

Lee contemplated his last forkful of rice and beans. One of the swarm of moths and less elegant creatures whirling about the coal oil lamp, a small grey-winged moth was perched on the forkful,

44

slowly raising and lowering its wings. Appeared to enjoy the capybara oil.

Had been a time Lee would have put that mouthful back onto the plate. That time was past.

Moth didn't taste like much. Hard for anything to taste like much in all that rat-grease.

"Yes," Lee said. "Run her on in."

"You don't kick her . . . you don't whip her." Bonifacia had become protective of the Indian girl, the bigger her belly grew. Lee supposed the kid was his. Wouldn't have cared to bet cash on it, though. He didn't fool himself that he was still anything but a half-stranger in this country yet. And that was as far as Argentina was concerned. The Chaco was yet another horse, an odder one. Only the jungle snakes, the monkey eagles, some few old witch women and ancient gauchos—only that crowd really knew this country.

"Run her in. I won't beat up on her. And take this plate away. I'd be mighty pleased if you didn't cook any more of those damn big rats. If you need beef, I'll have a side cut out for you."

Bonifacia made to spit into her hand, then apparently decided it was too much trouble to wash her hand again and refrained. "Too tough," she said. Fair enough, few Chacitas kept all their teeth. Lee supposed that giant rat was softer cooking and chewing than range beef.

"Too tough for you," Lee said. "O.K. for me."

"O.K.?" Bonifacia had never been sure about "O.K."

"Beef for me—capybara for the men."

45

A grunt. She picked up the plate, the coffee cup, and faded away out of the light. Lee supposed he could be fairly certain of more rat with his rice and beans. A woman who ran a house, usually *ran* the house, even if she was black, ancient, and one-eyed. Would have been smarter of him to demand capybara—would have gotten tough beef then and plenty of it.

Lee slid back the straw-bottom chair, got up with a grunt—it had been a long ride—and walked over to the *estancia's* single bed, a carved-headed double (from some Buenos Aires sporting house, Lee supposed) and the one item of value as furniture in the place. Lee had tried his damnedest to use the *hamacas,* the sleeping nets of the country, and found no rest at all to be gained from them, but only a mighty stiff back.

He had, therefore, after weeks of sad sleeping (which had left him seriously touchy—he had beaten a man named Alonso, and broken the fellow's left arm only because the man had spilled a drink of rum on Lee's boots in Pocito's) after these sleepless weeks, Lee had unhooked his hammock, rolled it, and thrown it out into the yard.

Then he had had toothless Arturo bring the wagon 'round, had climbed into it, and rattled away off the place which was then still becoming Stirrup, determined to find a bed.

He found it in Resistencia at a sale of a home for taxes, the home, apparently, having been a proper brothel—and further, one that boasted of furnishings purchased second hand from a grander establishment in the Capital. Found it, bought it at considerable expense, and had freighted it home in triumph.

Sweet sleep on a feather mattress had followed. He had broken no additional arms and had been accounted thereafter as a patient and even-tempered man.

Lee unbuckled his gunbelt, hung it at the ornate headboard, then unbuckled his trouser belt, stepped out of the baggy gaucho pantaloons (comfortable as the soft-top boots), and stripped off his shirt as well.

Tugged his socks off, then padded naked across the room and out the side door to the kitchen walk. Five big clay ollas hung from the walkway beams, their fat sides dewed with condensation. Lee reached up for one, lifted it down, set the round lid aside, then raised the heavy jar high over his head, tilted it, and poured a gallon and more of water down over his head, letting the water— not cool, to be sure, but perhaps slightly cooler than the air—course down his armpits, his chest and back. Would have to do until he got to the river tomorrow.

The Indian woman—a girl, really, Lee supposed, sixteen years old, or thereabouts— was sitting on the edge of the bed when he walked back into the shack. She was wearing, as usual, her best dress, a blue and white flour-sack thing, white ground, little blue flowers. Blue letters, *El Primo,* were printed across the material just at the bulge of her belly.

She had been an odd looking creature at her best—long, lank brown legs, calloused, splayed

Indian feet (no shoes on those feet, ever) a small, meagre ass on her, but considerable breasts, already sagging as if in anticipation of the coming years of brown sucklings and brute labor.

An almost handsome face, though. Almost noble, in its way. High-bridged, down-turned nose. Heavy lips, that might have been carved from the red quebracho—still had her teeth, too, though likely not much longer. Her eyes were flat out lovely. He'd noticed those eyes first of all, seeing her working laundry at the river—the sister of some woman on the place, some gaucho's sister-in-law, fresh from the forest—or almost fresh; someone had been into her before Lee. A calf's eyes, rich, brown, gentle.

"Take off your dress." Lee stood by the table, and turned up the wick on the coal oil lamp. Interested to see her more clearly . . . see how far she was along. Didn't care to be screwing the child right out of her all over his fine bed.

The Indian girl stood, docile as a pedigree dog, reached down past the mound of her belly to her dress's hem and pulled it up her body and then off, laying it carefully at the foot of the bed. Lee could see that she would have liked to fold it, but was afraid to delay.

She stood up straight so that he could see her clearly in the lamplight. She supposed, Lee thought, that he wished to do as he had been used to do—to examine her, to run his fingers through her hair for lice. And so he had, until he realized that these Chaco Indians were clean people, always washing in the river, rubbing their bodies with soap-root and bunch grass, always picking at each other like monkeys, and so stayed cleaner than the whites. Much cleaner.

She was. a wonderful thing to see, standing there, as Lee had always found women to be wonderful to see. Plain enough, he supposed to a man from Buenos Aires or Rio; would look to them more like an animal than a lady, standing there in lamplight made uncertain by the whirling, swarming insects that speckled and shadowed its throw of yellow light. There she was, brown as tanned leather, long-legged (her knees scarred from scrub work, from thorn) bare-footed, sway-backed both by nature and weight of her swollen belly poking out now fit to make her belly-button bulge, poking far enough to shadow slightly her small, fat split—that almost naked as a child's, after the fashion with Indian women, north or south.

Her tits hung slightly with the weight of anticipated milk, the nipples developed as if she'd suckled litters, the aureoles as big and dark brown as clay saucers.

Then, though, a pretty throat. A throat any lady (if it were a different color) would have been proud to show. Slender, round, lightly laced with delicate tendon, even finer veins, their traces barely visible beneath skin lightened to honey by its thinness. This slim neck, perfect as any woman's, held her head up as if it were presenting a gift to the sight of any man.

The solid Indian head . . . cheekbones polished by the tropic sun. Wonderful eyes. The hair like a waterfall of wet tar instead of water. Burnished, perfect black.

She was not, after all, entirely negligible.

Naked, Lee walked over to her, surprised as he always was by her slightness, by the slightness of most women once their clothes were off them and they stood close.

Lee put his hands on her arms, feeling their slimness, smooth skin, slender ropes of muscle.

Lifted the weight of her breasts in his hands, gently thumbed the nipples. Bent and took her right breast to his mouth, bit it, kissed it, then drew the soft neat strongly into his mouth. Suckled on her for a moment as if he were his own child, and felt her nipple slowly fatten on his tongue. The skin of her breast, as he pressed his face against her, smelled faintly of sweat and river water. Smelled of palm oil. No English Duchess, no New York Society woman had softer teats, sweeter, fatter nipples than these . . .

When he let loose of her, the Indian girl sighed, her breast shiny with his spittle, her nipple painfully swollen. Lee had thought he could taste her coming milk as he'd sucked and nursed at her. Thought he might bring that milk out yet, and before his baby came knocking for it, if he worked her hard enough, teased her as mares are teased sometimes to ready them for the stallion.

"Here," Lee said, and reached down, took her hands, and brought them up to his cock. He was swollen big as Aaron's rod. Big as bursting . . .

She stood as docile as she'd stood before, and held him in her two hands as a duffer might hold the handle of a baseball bat.

Always had to be told what to do, at least until the fit was on her; then she grunted, kicked, and flung with the best.

"Here, now." Lee put his hands onto her narrow shoulders—too narrow, it seemed, to hang such solid breasts from—and gently pushed her to sitting down on the edge of the mattress, so that his cock sprung nodding at her face. She looked at it, enigmatic, quiet, her fine mouth closed, until Lee touched her cheek with his hand, lightly ran his thumb across her lips. Then, as if she just now understood, Corazon opened her mouth, and as Lee guided her, his right hand clenched in her black hair, took his cock into her, her lips strained thin around it, her throat convulsing as he slowly, slowly forced the length of it deeper, over her trembling tongue . . . back, and further. Slowly, slowly, as she faintly whimpered, drawing snorting breaths, gagging . . . down into her throat.

He held it there, feeling the heat, the desperate fluttering struggle to accept it, to breathe despite it—looked down to see her dignity fled, all else fled except the stretched mouth, distorted face. The frantic, silent arching of her neck as he slowly pulled from her throat to let her breathe better, then, just as slowly, thrust back into her, holding her hands still where they might have dreamed of fighting against him.

She had done this for him once before and she knew how to do it. It was a question of relaxation. Of acceptance. Lee reached down to stroke her hair, thick and strong and black as a black mare's mane, to stroke her throat very lightly, his fingers tracing the tendons, the faint arteries swollen with her effort, that ran like tiny flower branches up the smooth column to the hollows of her ears. He caressed her so, gently, ran his finger tips along the tortured outlines of her lips, fluttering eyelids, the temples of her skull, tender under the dark curtain of her hair.

Then he gripped her by her hair again, held her still, and forced the bone-hard deeper.

She gagged and almost struggled then, but he held her still, and felt her, frantic, swallowing his meat. Swallowing it, and swallowing it and never getting it down.

She drew in a snorting breath and then another. And Lee felt her sag slightly under his hands, looked down and saw her dark-haired head, like a shot animal's, resting against him, her face against his crotch hair, his cock buried in her.

He lifted his hands from her, but the Indian girl didn't attempt to pull away, to disgorge him. Instead, she stayed, resting, softly snorting as she breathed—a full mouth, a full throat pulsing against what filled it, a jaw forced wide.

Looking down at her, feeling the narrow, moving heat against the head of his cock, the constriction and pressing there, feeling some faint movement of her trapped tongue against him, Lee saw, at either side of her dark head, her white-scarred knees wide spread in lamplight, spread wide as she sat, as if to echo her stretched mouth, her sprung jaws.

Lee kept her just that way for a minute and more and felt her softening, opening further, easing, slacking, all surrender now. Giving up everything for what he wished. Felt wetness—drops of spittle against his thigh.

He put his hands to her head again, gripped her, and slowly pulled his cock half out of her, felt her gulp, heave in a breath—and shoved it back into her mouth again, forcing it in all the way.

Then out, halfway. A wet, slippery sucking sound.

Then slowly into her throat again. Again the sound.

She moaned, her tongue twisted under it, and Lee, somewhat to his surprise, moaned loudly with her, pulled a painful sweetness up from his balls, and shot it into her mouth, down her convulsing throat, bucking and groaning with the great pleasure of it as she gulped and gulped, swallowing, fighting for breath, moaning with him as if they were trying to remember a song.

It took a while for the pleasure to become less. A while that was a pleasure in itself.

When he pulled away from her, he was still dripping, the cream still oozing from him. She stared at it in the flickering lamplight, breathing hoarsely, face dewed with sweat, her hair, sweat-soaked, hanging half across her face.

She put a hand up to hold the softening thing; her other hand stayed tucked down between her thighs, as if for safe-keeping. She held Lee's cock for a moment, then looked up at him to see what he wished her to do. Lee said nothing to her . . .

stood silent, listening to the slowing beats of his heart.

She squeezed at the shaft that had been choking her before, and now was pliant, diminishing. Then she did without prompting what she wished to do, and leaned a little forward, cautiously, over the small bulk of her belly, and commenced to lick at him just as a cat cleansed her kittens after play. Licking at the wet, sucking at the oily tip as simply as a child sucked at candy, to get it all. Then, her dark hair swaying, her head nodding as she drew her tongue up the wet length of it, licking along, then back to lick up the shaft again.

Considerably to his surprise since he had felt near killed coming into her, Lee felt his cock jump slightly in her hands. Then, as the girl continued in that way of cleansing, swallowing sometimes, as if time had passed, or a different girl had come into the room. He grew hard in her hand . . . felt her hesitate in her licking, her gentle sucking at it.

"All right, then. Do you want it so . . . ?"

He'd spoken to her in English, though, and the girl didn't understand him. She looked up, then went back to what she'd been doing. Seemed to please her to use her tongue in that fashion.

Lee reached down and gently pushed her away from him, gently pushed her back down onto the bed. She lay as still as a sheep to be slaughtered, and Lee had an instant uncomfortable notion of some odd men's reasons for murdering girls. Her posture seemed to expect it in some way, as if stabbing (and then, perhaps, cooking and devouring her) would be as natural a thing to accomplish as any other penetration. She lay spraddled, sprawled, her long legs akimbo to show the notched pout between them, almost bare of fur. Her breasts, heavy, swollen soft, lolled each to the side a little with their weight. She looked up at him from the rumpled shelter of her long black hair as simply as an animal might have. But Lee was not such a fool as to think that anything but impression, whatever the gauchos thought.

He had known Indians before.

Her belly was mounded up as she lay—wasn't likely she could take much weight upon it.

Lee leaned down and slapped her flank.

"Turn over," he said.

Obedient as any nigger slave, the girl turned on her belly, showing Lee her meagre ass, her long, strong brown legs. The black, smooth fall of her hair.

Lee, still something surprised to be hard as a horse-rail after such a draining, swung up on the bed to kneel above her, reached down, hooked his hands under the angles of her hips, and lifted her ass up into the air, so that she lay braced there on her knees beneath him, her long black deep curved line of spine shadowed in lamplight, her face buried in her folded arms amidst the pillows.

Lee, his cock aching as if nothing had been taken from it in a month, knelt back a bit, slid his hands from her hips to her buttocks, gripped them, and pulled them gently apart, splitting her, displaying what she had. Almost no hair at all there—strange that the savage Indians, supposedly so rough, so near the beast, should have less fur about them in private places. Though that was true, too, of Oriental women . . . true of Chinese girls, at any rate.

True of Chinese girls . . .

Lee gently stroked a finger up the Indian's warm crack. Up from the soft groove of her cunt (hanging slightly open, now, from her posture, leaving the slightest trace of moisture at his fingertip) on up from there to damp, sweaty skin, the curves of her buttocks warm against the sides of his hand, and slowly, gently, on up to the dark, wrinkled little dimple of her ass.

He stroked her again, even more gently, more slowly. Felt, this time, more moisture from her, then gripped her buttocks harder than he had before, pulled them apart and saw her cunt half sprung open by this, a slice of its wet showing, a small slice of wet red shining in yellow coal oil light.

Lee put a finger to her there, then slid it in as she grunted. Slid it high up into the slippery— wedged in another finger, and heard her grunt again. He'd heard that this late along, women carrying had differences in their insides. Heard that, but it didn't appear to be so, though perhaps it was, higher than a finger or two could reach.

If so, he had the reacher—though he wouldn't care to do her any hurt.

Lee pulled his fingers out of her, felt the girl's warm, bare ass move against him as if she'd rather have kept them there, then placed his forefinger, still wet enough against the button of her ass, turned it in a slow corkscrewing motion, and shoved it up into her.

The girl jerked away—or tried to—and cried out something in Indian. She half turned on the bed and put a hand back, almost as if to touch him, to try and push him away.

Lee leaned over and slapped her, once, across the side of her face, and she turned back and was still. Appeared, though, she didn't care for any ass-fucking notion, with child or not, and Lee couldn't see himself the sort of man to force it upon her, and her likely carrying his own.

He left the finger in her there, though, for a moment, and slowly turned it, opening her a little, easing her tightness before he pulled it free. With his other hand, he had commenced to stroke the long muscles of her back, gentling her, calming her as he would have a mare too nervous for some necessity.

"If you don't want it, then you shan't have it, Little Mother," he said to her, and stroked and caressed along that smooth, warm skin, faintly damp with sweat, smelling slightly of fish from where his fingers had first been . . . slightly of palm oil from her hair. She moved slightly under his hand as he stroked her, like a cat unused to caresses.

Lee reached down, gripped his cock, and brought the tip of it up to her, up between her legs to nudge at the soft place . . . to find the wet, narrow slickness of her cunt. Pushed there, and in, just the slightest bit. The Indian arched her back . . . held still.

Lee shoved it into her—felt something different as he thrust, more slipperyness . . . more squeezing. The girl grunted as she took him; Lee felt her tremble under his weight as his cock rode up into her all the way. Felt different, no doubt about it. Narrower . . . tighter.

He pulled out a little way, the pulling out feeling every bit as good as the thrusting into her had done. She was oily enough to grease a mechanism . . . lay, face buried in the pillows, buttocks high to accomodate him, presenting like a cow . . . a mare in heat. Her gash was wide open, now, slick red in the lamplight where his cock stuck deep into her. She made some sort of a whining noise as he bucked up into her again, riding the rod all the way with a soft sucking sound. He put his hands down to grip her slender thighs as he fucked into her . . . felt the long wrapped muscles there clench to bear him as he drove into her again, pulled the length of his cock almost out of her, hesitated— then drove it in.

Leaning over her, socketed in all the way, Lee saw the soft outer round of her right breast, brown against the rough white cotton sheet, bulge slightly as he came forward onto her, the wet noise came from their joining, and he put his arm down to brace, to keep their weight off her belly.

Thought of being gentler but it wasn't what she wanted; she shoved her butt back into him now every time the cock went into her . . . said something in Indian.

Slaves or Indians, whores or whatever, in

whichever sort of situation they found themselves bedded, there came the time they called for what they wanted as imperious as any queen. And so, grunting as he struck deeper into her now, swaying from the impact of the thrusts, the weight of her belly, her shaking thighs spread wide under him, her slight buttocks raised high to present her soaking cunt, constantly transfixed, Corazon insisted on her fill, grunted and whimpered for it, shoved her ass back into Lee to receive it, and turned him from served into server.

These demonstrations of women's pleasures had never troubled Lee—in fact had always pleased him, and did so now. His cock, hard as hard wood, seemed to try to tug his jism from him at each stroke, and faster and stronger as the girl groaned beneath him.

"Oh, you darling," Lee said, no more foolishly than most men in such a state to most women, whatever their color. "Ahh—you darling . . . !"

The girl snarled underneath him, her face turned in the pillows, turned into the lamplight.

There was an odd expression on her face. Lee supposed it was pleasure.

THREE

Three days later, a gaucho named Narçicito found two of Lee's beeves dead with broken necks. Their guts had been eaten out.

"Oh, no!" Arturo had said, upon his discovery, very pleased. *"El Tigre!"* Had said this in his liquid way, toothless gums plastered with coca leaf and tobacco mixed, and had clapped his big hands together, hands as hard-calloused as a pony's hooves making a sound loud as a pistol shot.

He and the other men had looked at Lee as hound puppies might with a hunt in promise— visions of galloping into the Mato with their new Winchesters (those splendid gifts of so splendid a *Patron*) to hunt the jaguar down, and, in the most heroic manner, shoot it to bits—each, somehow, to return in triumph with the whole glorious hide to himself.

Such a hunt would take a day or two at least— perhaps more, if the big cat faded back deeper into the forest. Two days, perhaps more, of no cattle moving, no fence post digging, no ditch cleaning, no wire stringing, no scooping out of worm cysts and pouring in of idioform. None, in fact, of any of the routines of labor.

They were like children, wanting such a holiday.

Lee and his men were sitting their horses, smoking, beside the slaughtered beeves. One steer here, the other lying some yards away.

This was open country—a fair mile above the ox-bow where the Paraña curved around and past Juan Soto's store and barrelhouse. Soto's was located more or less (depending on the river's stage of flood) on Lee's land, though neither he nor Soto had ever chosen to make an issue of it. That parcel was too wet, even for Chaco steers, to be of much ranching use, and Soto's—as a shanty at which to get a drink of rum, a game of cards, some trouble or some cheap woven-rope tack— was a useful station (and temptation) for Lee's gauchos. Orellana's men, too. A gaucho dead drunk at Soto's was at least handy to the estancia. A gaucho dead drunk in Resistencia was a loss for a week.

This stretch also, where the jaguar had come hunting, must have been not too long ago a flood plain for the river. The country was open, wide, spreading away from them two miles east to the river, nearly a mile due north to a line of *chonta* palms, more than a mile in a great semi-circle south and west.

All Stirrup land and fine grazing. *Tlictuk* grass, the Indians called it. Shoulder high to a horse and wider in the leaf than bunch grass, thicker than gramma. Tasted bitter to Lee when he'd first tried it—the Indian name meant that, apparently—but the cattle liked it well enough. Horses, of course, were spoiled on alfalfa down here . . .

It was hotter than blazes today. Hotter than hell below Texas. To the north, the line of palms shimmered in the heat, a duplicate line of palms trembling in the afternoon's worst heat down here —mirages more clear, more convincing than even those Lee had seen at sea.

The carcass, half buried in the deep grass, was being buried again, as Lee looked at it, by a living black blanket of flies. The flies would have their day or two, then the maggots would blossom in the thing. The cat had twisted the steer's neck back, then broken it. Must have gone for the other animal just after. Damn fool beef to have lingered at such a scene.

The jaguar had left the first kill at a hard run— the pug marks, some of them, still visible amid crushed grass stems. Caught up the second animal, mounted it, and broke its neck.

Cat hadn't troubled with beef, had been happy enough to tear out innards and eat them. And a damn big cat. A good deal bigger than the biggest cougar Lee had ever seen. "Almost three hundred pounds of cat," Arturo had said, smacking his hands together.

"Do we hunt, *Patron?*"

It was a temptation to let them loose, if only for the pleasure of seeing *their* pleasure, seeing them dash, yelping, stunting off their saddles. A temptation.

"No," Lee said. "If I lose madmen like you into the *Mato,* there wouldn't be a *tigre* alive from Acunsión to Sante Fe—and this in addition to the

rape of every *Indio* you can get a *bola* cord or
—men's work, not suited to Indians like Martín or
smiles he'd wanted. No man minded being
thought a devil of a fellow.

"Beside which, there is serious work to be done
—men's work, not suited to Indians like Martín or
Louis." These last were elderly Javanches—
brothers, likely—who Juan McGee had gifted Lee
with at the time of the land sale. The gift had been
in the nature of a practical joke; the two old
cannibals good for nothing, really, except
skimping chores and eating a hundred pounds of
red beans between them every four months. "This
work with the cattle can not wait and will not
wait."

The gauchos sighed a collective disappointed
sigh and slumped in their saddles, but they did not
argue as Idaho drovers would have done. Individ-
ually savage fellows, they had too serious a view
of social position to dream of telling their *Patron*
to take a trot.

"El Tigre . . . ?" Arturo—a disrespectful
Italian grandfather perhaps prompting the
question.

"I'll hunt the cat," Lee said, "if you believe
yourself capable of commanding the tasks on this
estancia for the next two days."

A nice question. Lee had learned *something* of
handling these men. Arturo was intelligent enough
to be a fair foreman, if not left to it for too long a
time. And the only man dangerous enough to give
him trouble, fat Nacio Fortún, was providentially
his brother-in-law, and therefore slightly less

likely than most to stick a knife into him if Arturo chose to give a tiresome order.

Arturo considered Lee's question, champing his lank and toothless jaws as he did it, an aid to ratiocination. Lee saw Fat Nacio grinning at him over Arturo's shoulder. Nacio was no fool—and less a fool now, since Lee had clipped his ear.

"I will undertake the responsibility," Arturo said, as if he'd been offered the Presidency of the country, and Lee leaned from the saddle to shake the gaucho's hand (felt like shaking a pony's hoof).

"I trust you," Lee said, and that was that. The other gauchos satisfied, as well—if there was to be no hunt, there would at least be drama: Arturo, as *Jefe*. And Lee as well—a chance to try a man who might relieve him on another, perhaps more important occasion. The *Patron* had been playing first and second fiddle for long enough.

"Very well," Lee said. "Leave one of the carrions. The cat might come back tonight; it's worth trying." He eased the dun away from the carcass; horse wasn't caring for the stink. "Now we have calves to catch. Let's get on with it."

It would be an embarrassment if he didn't now kill that damned cat. It would also be expensive. If the jaguar chose to raid in this territory long enough, he could cut out and kill many hundreds of pesos' worth of beef. It was not a loss Lee could afford.

It was not a loss he was prepared to afford.

There'd been a man named Cruçero, a small, restless fellow with an Indian wife and seven children to feed. Cruçero had been a cotton picker, and had probably found the work—backbreaking at best—very distasteful at temperatures of one hundred and fourteen Fahrenheit. He had stolen one of Stirrup's steers, skinned it, and butchered it out. He and his family had had at least one good dinner from that beef before Lee and two of his men rode into their clearing.

It was a problem. Difficult to simply whip a rustler senseless down here, peel some skin off the fellow's back, reveal a little rib, and drop the matter there.

Difficult. Men in Argentina often lived in dreams of their own lives. Men of that sort couldn't bear insults unavenged. There was, therefore, only one manner of handling these poor, proud, and foolish men.

Lee had called Cruçero out, and the man had fortunately came to his doorstep with an old Martini-Henry carbine in his hands. Relieved, Lee had made a slow, deliberate show of drawing the Bisley Colt's—gave the fellow a world of time to try and level his piece. Then, as Cruçero finally got his bead, had shot him through the head from horseback and nearly forty feet away. It had been a considerable feat, had ended the affair decently, and had since, no doubt, saved Lee much expense in steer stealing.

Only man Lee had had to kill in this country—excepting the pimp, Sarmiento.

After the event, Lee had sent a rider to that clearing (on Philipe Orellana's land, as it happened) every week, with beans, rice, and sun-dried beef for Cruçero's woman and her children. This had been regarded as odd behavior in a land-owner, particularly in a Chaco land-owner. Odd, but not dishonorable.

The moon came up late, crescent the shape and color of a slice of tangerine.

A breathless night, and just as well. Lee had no notion of being pleased by playing ring-around-the-rosy, quartering a shifting wind with a jaguar. Doing that sort of dance, circling a rotting carcass in near darkness, seemed a good way to get clawed to rags.

Better to sit tight with no wind at all. Better to squat in high grass with a Winchester across your knee, the murdered beef barely visible two dozen yards away. Would be better still if the mosquitos hadn't found Lee an hour before—had been biting on him in clouds ever since. He'd thought he'd experienced mosquitos up in the States. Been mistaken about that for sure; this country was the heart and heaven of the breed.

Lee left the dun a mile and more back country, tethered to clump of wild grape. He would be cutting quite a figure if the jaguar were to circle that far south, kill his horse for him while he sat lookout in high grass over spoiled steaks.

He hadn't hunted all that much in recent years —had had a fine, sad, last pleasure-hunt one winter in the Rockies. Had killed a perfect elk then and decided against any more hunting for pleasure. Hunted for food, of course, since. Food and necessity, like this stand-hunt for the cat.

Lee'd seen jaguars twice. One animal, a big female, shot and dead in the market at Tucuman. The other cat had been alive—might, in fact, be this very one he was waiting for. Twenty miles up the Paraña, one early misty morning—was the first time he'd gotten up the nerve to club and cook an *iguana* lizard for his breakfast. Taken considerable sand, that had, though it turned out well enough. Tasted like prairie hen, if you were careful not to remember too clearly what prairie hen had tasted like, slow roasted over hickory coals.

On that morning, after finishing up what he could bring himself to carve out of that damn ugly iguana, he had walked out of camp a little way to shit and, having dropped his trousers and squatted, was rewarded for his carelessness in not scouting a bit by the sight of the hugest damned wild cat he had ever seen. Dark, dark rich gold in the pelt, splashed all over like a painter's dream with rosettes as big, black and soft-looking as could be.

This cat, this *tigre,* big, wide-chested, heavy-pawed, was padding down along the river bank— looked, from its attention, to be fishing (for all the world like some grizzly bear searching for summer salmon), staring down into the ripples with eyes like topaz gems . . . occasionally patting at the water with its right forepaw in a tentative fashion. Didn't appear to be cautious of water, though, like most cats—plunged right into a shallow bow, and paddled upstream as easy as a beaver. Heaved out, shook itself like a dog, and came pacing past the thicket where Lee, quiet as a fieldmouse, squatted undignified and still as stone. Didn't fancy being slashed to bits while screeching in terror, fumbling amid the folds of his fallen trousers for his holstered revolver.

That would be a sad end, indeed.

Lee never knew if the animal sensed he was there—certainly would have if Lee'd already commenced his shitting before the big cat came along. Even so, the cat might have known . . . simply not been interested in so foreign a smell, so odd a presence at this *Norte Americano*, crouched in the Paraña roughs in a sweat of fear.

Whichever, the jaguar had passed on by.

Indians would say Lee owed the spirit of those cats a mighty favor. And the Indians would be right, Lee supposed. But white men were notoriously ungrateful for that sort of blessing, and Lee intended to lose no more beef. Not if he could make a decent shot by dark moonlight.

Time . . . time. Lee sat, trying to ease the stiffening muscles of his back without moving, thinking on the nature of time. It took so little of it to let a bullet pass through a few feet of air . . . to cross some smoky room. Took a great deal of time, though, waiting for something, waiting for somebody you cared to see.

And if you were never to see them again?

Then waiting took the most time of all.

Some sleepy *hornero* called across the grass, and Lee sat up straighter, slid his hand down the Winchester's stock. The moonlight ran like

69

Chilean wine, light red and soaking, down through the tall grass stems. Like Chilean wine or watered blood. The color was rich enough so that a man might almost expect warmth from it, as though the crescent moon had become some smaller nighttime sun.

This country had its beauties—odd, and dangerous as its fat and murderous little piranha fish, its great snakes, thick through the body as a ship's cable. Beauties of weather, too—furnace weather with sunsets, sunrises of fire.

Would have liked S'eon to see this country . . .

Lee's backside was beginning to ache from such a long sit-down—two, three hours now, maybe longer. Also wished he hadn't considered snakes. It would be comic ill luck to be sitting stand for a jaguar, only to have some fér-de-lance or bushmaster slide out of the grass to bite him on the butt and put him under. Would mean leaving this life as only a joke, to make men grin over their rum.

It was more than possible the cat wasn't coming. A good deal more than possible. Also possible that if the animal waited much longer, there wouldn't be enough moon left to shoot by. And to miss him here meant going over the river after him, into the *Mato*. Likely to the falls past Paracaçu. Big cats coming through the country were mostly said to den there.

Lee had ridden down to Paracaçu once with Juan McGee and a gaucho named Porfirio. They'd been scouting timber and had found giant fig trees, one hundred, two hundred feet tall, and bigger around than a forty-foot lasso would stretch. There'd been ironwood, rosewood, mahogany . . .

No way to get the stuff out, though. The falls at Paracaçu proved too steep, too various, too narrow for rafting such mighty timbers to the Paraña. Lee'd had to do with lumber transport before in a small way, and this difficulty was plain to see, and inescapable.

A rich resource, and no way to get it onto the river and so raft to the mills. Resource and no transport. Almost the history of the Chaco right there—though now, of course, the railroad made a difference at least for the stockmen and farmers.

The falls had been beautiful, and swarming with butterflies in colors of azure and vivid pink, sulfur yellows, and creams light and airy as a lady's skin. Very beautiful. A swift series of narrow fall after fall, cascade and shower, splash and run, all in a thunder of sound, soft crashes . . . surrounded by the *Mato* tree limbs enfolding, bending all in various green. *Caiman* in the larger pools as the water descended, their slender crocodile snouts just visible above the rippling surfaces.

They'd found jaguar scat there, Porfirio judging the sex and size of the cat as neatly as any Crow could judge of a painter.

S'eon would have so enjoyed that place . . . the butterflies . . .

Any woman would. Catherine Dowd . . . any of the women Lee had known. It was a feature of growing older, he'd found, that a man became lonelier, no matter what his company might presently be. He'd lost all those people of the past, was the reason for that solitude.

Difficult for present company to make up for that company of the used-to-be. Couldn't make up for them, really. Odd too, that among those people so missed not only the loved were there, but men Lee'd killed. Men and women he'd not cared for at all. Was as if simply being remembered gave them value.

Wouldn't mind—though he'd never have thought it before—wouldn't mind having Harvey Logan sitting here tonight in Chaco grass beside him. That neat, bright, and murderous little man . . .

Or blowhard George Peach. Lee'd had no business killing George, had known it right afterward. That was a boy's business of fist-fight and wrestle in the alley. Or should have been. Lee doubted that boys that age had any right at all to be carrying deadly weapons. Couldn't see as they had caused anything but trouble, to men so young, so raw and stupid.

Wouldn't mind having old George right here, right now.

Wouldn't mind having any of them, those *past* people, alive and keeping him company down here in Argentina. What a fine fancy fandango of a time they'd all have in this wild country! Not like the West, now, closing in, closing down to the telegraph and the railroad trains.

They'd all have a hell of a time down here. Blackie, to run a saloon for the boys . . . that slender pimp, the razor man, "Harry" something, to run some girls. What the hell had been that one-eyed girl's name? Had he ever heard her name?

And his father.

More than any of them except the Chinese girl, he'd like his father here, sitting still in Chaco grass by moonlight, waiting for a cat. "Wonderfully dangerous men . . ." old Bonifacia had said of the great gauchos, all dead now. She would have been certainly pleased with Buckskin Frank Leslie. Would have been pleased as punch with Lee's daddy, would have fed him great lashings of roasted rat and rice. Lee's father would have eaten the stuff, and then gone out to the kitchen walk to thank her as if she were white, and a lady.

Bonifacia would have been more than satisfied with *that* dangerous man.

Lee straightened his back a little as he sat, trying to ease it, heard the whine of the swarming mosquitos alter in his ears as he moved that little bit—and, so, by that instant's inattention, didn't see the jaguar come.

The cat was suddenly on the carcass—big, soft gold in the moonlight, its broad head bent to eat.

Lee raised the Winchester—the jaguar's head came up instantly with that movement—and Lee shot it as it leaped away, light as air, into deeper dark.

Lee'd heard the "thump," though, as it went. The .44 slug striking home. But not into bone, not into the heart or lungs.

He'd fired too late. Been too busy dreaming, acting the fool for memory.

Lee stood, let the Winchester fall, and drew his Colt's. If it came at him now, there'd be no time for riflery.

Silence; no wind, no movement in the tall grasses. Only the smothering heat. Clouding mosquitos whining in his ears. The stink of the dead steer.

Come to me, now, Lee said to the Jaguar, but silently, in his mind. *Come to me, now, and let us settle this.*

The big cat badly hurt, for sure. Even a fool's rifle can do some work.

Come on to me now, big, handsome, yellow cat . . .

Tell the truth and shame the devil—it had startled him. Scared him. He'd stopped expecting it, and suddenly there the damn thing had been, and big as a house.

Silence . . . except for that same bird. Calling now in answer to the sound of the shot, likely.

Lee slowly turned clear 'round, had visions of the wounded cat circling, circling. Damn thing had had a head big as a bear's . . .

"All right," Lee said out loud, his voice sounding mighty foreign in the night. "All right, now—come on or get to running; it's all the same to me!"

Silence. Faint moon-shadows drifting across the grass. It was getting darker, clouding up. The *hornero* called again, more distant. Lee stood, his revolver cocked and ready, and listened. Bird must be flying down toward the river. Be nice to think the jaguar was already heading that way, back hunched with the pain of its wound, the bullet into its belly, Lee thought, or hindquarters.

A mighty hunter—a Nimrod, for sure—standing for a cat through half the night, then missing the creature's vitals at a stone's throw.

Mighty hunter . . .

"The hell with you!" Lee said, bent down to find the Winchester, picked it up with his left hand, then started off striding through the grass, careless of the noise he made. The cat, if he were still near, would know where Lee was in any case once he'd fired that shot, moved.

It would be a long walk in near dark through high grass to reach the dun. Then, presuming the *tigre* didn't come for him from the grass while he walked, there would be a long ride down to the river. A pause while Sanchez was wakened to rope-and-pully the little one-horse ferry across, then another ride into the afternoon down to the falls at Paracaçu. Where the jaguar *might* have denned again, if it had rested there before . . . if it was not too badly hurt to travel so far, if it didn't change its mind . . .

The Yankee cowboy had missed his shot, was the fact of it. And had a wounded cat to show. A cat that, crippled, might turn to hunting humans —women doing their wash by the river, children playing in the scrub—if he weren't found and finished.

By the man responsible.

He rode down the last stretch of trail (though called a trail only by courtesy) in the oven heat of late afternoon, through a chanted chorus of monkey calls from the towering walls of green on either side of the narrow outcrop of crumbling stone that made even this much of a trail possible. If not for that, Lee would have had to dugout down river, tie up, then walk into the *Mato,* guided only by the sounds of the falls where the unnamed small tributary looped through forest, then dropped steeply down to rejoin the Paraña.

The dun, worn by the heat, was nervous of the forest, half shying at every fruit-bat, crab-spider or parrot that rustled in the foliage which rose as seeming solid as any building of irregular stone (but all the shades of green), two hundred feet high on either side of them, and often crowding so close that Lee could spread his arms out to touch both at once.

At such places, where the jungle walls almost closed in, the great treetops met high above, and ceilinged out the sun as perfectly as a slate roof might have done, so that Lee rode his horse for those hundreds of yards along a narrow track in evening.

To be oppressed by so much green, (so much rustling, creeping, calling life) was, Lee thought, much what living under the sea must be. Green, and lacking light. Restless, lovely, and full of every sort of sudden peril.

Cuchillo's villages were on this side of the river. And Cuchillo had lost a man only a few days before. Lost him to Lee.

It was true the Indian might not know it was Lee personally had killed the fellow. True also, Cucillo

might not know that Lee had now crossed the river
. . . was hunting a hurt cat at the run of the falls at
Paracaçu.

Might be a perfectly ignorant savage.

Might be.

And if he was, would be the first such red man
that Lee had ever heard of. And in his home
woods, too.

A sensible thing would be to get this business
done and over and to get, thereafter, back across
the river with no time lost. It would be even more
sensible, or course, to cut his losses with that
damned jaguar, turn the dun's head upstream,
and take a run-out powder pronto.

Awkward to explain to the men, to be sure.
Have to wind a considerable ball of yarn to wrap
that story in.

*Shot the cat, lost it in the pool below the falls?
Shot the cat—but was driven off by* Indios *before
it could be skinned?*

Neither tale seemed likely to wash.

Truth was, he owed the world that damned cat,
owed it doubly now that he had maimed the thing.
Simplest just to pay what he owed and not figure
lies about why he didn't.

The dun, a strong-backed little horse (too small
for Lee's length of leg, was the truth), was picking
his way as light as he could step over the
crumbling marly stone, his hide twitching in fly-
jerks at every touch of frond or leaf along his sides
as he went. Unhappy horse. The smell, Lee
supposed, was upsetting him as much as any odd
noises, scuttlings, the dimness, the sudden blaze of

sun through the canopy high, high above. The forest smelled like a fat, dreadful thing, half plant and half not—rotting dead.

Were it not for the growing noise of the falls, their succession of silver sounds, of drum sounds to his right, Lee would long since have feared he might be lost, trail or no trail. Such lonely, narrow ledges of weak stone—the remnant of great ridges worn and broken and eaten away by the forest— might meander anywhere, and nowhere. Might support a horseman along for many miles, branching, turning, intersecting, turning back and doubling again through pillars of green and walls of green and courtyards of green until there was no longer any true turning to be found—or known, if it could be found.

Lee listened carefully to the falls on his right. He had no Juan McGee, no half-breed Porfirio to show him his way home.

Falls on the right to arrive. Falls on the left for the ride back up the ferry. Would do to keep that in mind, whatever happened.

Beside the jaguar. Besides the Indians.

Falls on the right to arrive—on the left to get home.

FOUR

He rode out to the bank of that small, nameless river, that steep little river, more than an hour later. At forty-three minutes past three o'clock by his silver-backed stem-winder.

This section was wide, the soft stone of the trail stretching to a shelf some twenty feet across, perhaps twice that in length along the torrent. This rock shelf was wet from spray, misty and cool, which came booming over it in quick surges from the cataract that spilled from a height above to funnel down with force and shatter on the stones that once had been part of this same shelf, before the water wore them down and broke them.

There, Lee was cooler than he had been in some months, and swung down off the dun to stand at its head, being dampened and enjoying it. Coolest he'd been in a hell of a time.

Shirt finally soaked, trousers soaked, Lee led the dun back into the *Mato* a little way, tied him to a shade-stunted chonta, loosed his girth, slid the Winchester out of its saddle bucket, and left the horse, already lonely and yearning, to roll an eye after him as he shoved through the growth back to the roar and boom, the cool, blowing, rainy air of the falls.

The gaucho had called the third cataract the place where the big cats denned—solitary, to be sure—as they passed, hunting, through territories half the size of Yankee states.

The third cataract would make for a considerable climb down over rock fragments, snags, the splintered trunks of larger trees torn loose from the forest upstream—ripped out by the roots, picked up, spun, splintered, and thrown down here, their backs broken, however hard the wood might be.

There, and slick stone slippery as ice to climb down.

It would be one of the poorest places for a man to break his leg. Lee had heard of a fellow that broke his leg in a horse-fall in Paraguay, and so lay crippled in the path of driver ants—in fact, had likely seen that huge, red swarming ball of ants, a full ten, twelve feet high, slowly begin to melt for their migration, slowly turn into a small river of orange-red, flowing over everything in its path, rippling toward this unfortunate like a tide of constant tiny things with tiny jaws. And so the poor cripple, too slow to crawl out of the way, was drowned and devoured as he lived, the stream of ants receding finally, ebbing away through his polished bones, while parrots still answered his screams from far away.

Decidedly, the *Mato Grasso* was no stead in which to break a leg.

Lee climbed down carefully, the Winchester

slung across his back by its single-strand rawhide sling, the keeper loop pushed down the Bisley's hammer. Would be unwise to lose either piece.

The third cataract was almost as Lee remembered it—smaller, though, the banks of the stream closer than he'd recalled.

He lay flat on his belly just above, looking down at the place, trying where he might get a bead into the long, flat rock shelves, the shallow, water-hollowed niches the falls had carved across the stream. Here, the water was diverted into various torrents, some thunderous, some less so, and many of these had in times of flood struck across the stone formation opposite, hitting it high where the jungle left the rock exposed and cutting long, horizontal trenches, boring out those holes, those natural dens.

On this side of the river, just below him, Lee saw nothing but jungle over a receding bank. The ledges of stone were all across the stream, and that was certainly where the cat was laired—if it had been here at all, if it was such a creature of habit as gossip had it.

Lee could see no better place to be than where he was, perhaps back a little, under the broad leaves of a shrub, under some shelter from the rain of mist always ghosting down. Still keeping flat, he inch-wormed back into the green, to be slightly dryer, to keep his guns from being soaked, then checked to see that he still had his look-out over the whole range of worn stone opposite. Did that injured son-of-a-bitch come home, he was dead meat.

* * *

It proved a long wait.

Damned long.

Lee waited, lying flat on damp, cool stone as the afternoon faded like an old Daguerreotype. Faded and faded away in bird calls, the sobbing cries of some lonely monkey on some thick-leaved branch a long pistol-shot above the forest floor.

Lee had never taken his eyes from those shelves, those dens of rock across the stream; the Winchester, levered and cocked, rested in his hands, cool, damp, patient with the patience of all machinery. Lee had not looked about for snakes, or bird-eating spiders. Nor centipedes, either. He'd watched the dens.

There would not be another too-late shot.

He watched until nightfall. Watched until he couldn't see even the outlines of the ledges over there, until even a jaguar's golden hide might as well be a panther's sooty black.

Then, still not searching for varmints, not troubling himself about them, he slowly backed deeper into the forest, to be further sheltered from that cold spray and mist that had some time ago ceased to be a pleasure. Crawled back slowly . . . slowly in the darkness, lifting the cold length of the Winchester so that not a touch of steel on stone might sound, until he lay half-buried in foliage as thick and thickly leaved as any privet hedge, curled up like a dog on a fireside rug, cradling the rifle—and went to sleep.

A long, long, sweet sleep, as if he rested on feather down in a fine New York hotel. No dreams. No dreams at all that he could remember.

He woke shaking with cold in early morning darkness and crawled slowly out of the leaf-soggy, mold-soggy place he had slept, back out onto the stone ledge, sliding slowly on his belly in the misty wet, shallow puddles here and there where the falls had splashed high as he slept.

There were several moments before Lee could hear the fall's thundering—his ears had closed to that constant battering in the night.

The moon was down. Only a surging suggestion of whiteness, a racing, roaring ghost of white went foaming past him as he lay flat on his belly, slid the Winchester (the weapon as wet as he was) up and ready, its barrel resting on his left forearm and eared back the rifle's hammer to full cock.

So, lying there, shivering from chill water, an ache across the small of his back as if a man had kicked him in a fight, Lee waited for the light and moved not another inch this way or that.

The river's dash and spray collected in the curl of his sombrero and slowly dripped from there as he lay. Lee watched through the darkness to the other darkness across the torrent, waiting. A hundred yards . . . not much more than that. A good range for the Winchester, which ran out of breath at three hundred. Would have been nothing, of course, for a Sharps, but that slow and mighty piece was one a man hardly saw anymore. Lee supposed that now he would miss the fast repeating. Machines quickening everything—even killing, which before had always seemed to come more than quick enough to most men.

He watched the dark across the river and

wondered if the wounded cat could have come this far. It was, Lee thought, a fair time yet 'till dawn. He wasn't impatient for it, however. He was very willing to wait. Waiting had become an odd pleasure for him. Would be willing to wait for however long it took. For that, the *Mato* was perfect. In patience, it was no "Green Hell" at all. It was a medicine for waiting . . .

At half light—only half-light, and most of that brought down into the rapids' pitch by the silver of the flowing water, the ivory foam as it struck rocks, Lee saw his vision of rock shelves, rock ledges, rock hollows only marked with vines and creepers, intruded upon. The jaguar, gathering light to its golden hide, walked, not lame, deliberate as could be onto the place where Lee was looking. It stretched a heavy paw down out of a tangle of green and emerged, the rest of its body following that first paw-pad like bright honey syrup poured from a jug of green. Its head, broad as it was long, swung slowly from side to side as it paced out upon the ledge. Lee stopped his breath and laid a bead as neat as fine stitching just behind the breast's right shoulder as it walked. The cat paused, and looked up into the trees as if it were watching for the morning's arrival, and Lee squeezed off his shot, sent the bullet where he'd aimed it, and knocked the animal down.

The jaguar skidded sideways on the stone, found its footing and bounded up the sheer face of rock toward the next highest ledge, caught that edge, clung for an instant, and received Lee's second shot into its broad back. High, between the great wings of its shoulder blades.

This bullet broke its back, and the cat, clinging, knowing Lee's direction now, turned its head to stare across the torrent at him. Its eyes were green as glass.

Lee levered the rifle's mechanism, wounded the animal's fine back again, and killed it.

Nimrod, Lee thought. The mighty hunter.

It was no joke at all, crossing that stream.

Lee went downstream first, on his side, looking for some ford that wouldn't kill him. He found a possible two pistol-shots further down, left the Winchester there against a fig tree bole, slid and stomped and skidded down to the rapids' edge, then marched on in, feeling his boots fill to icy lead . . . feeling the water kicking and punching at him. Shoving, trying to kick him off his feet and down, so it could roll him under, hold him under. Break his face on rocks.

Shallow, though. Shallow right here over a shelf of stone the size of a house roof. All well enough, if a man wasn't to slip on the slick, on the water mosses. If a man wasn't that sort of a fool as to slip and fall.

The water rushed smooth and clear as thicker air around Lee's legs. He wished to God he'd thought to take his boots off, leave them with the rifle. Might have been more slippery, though, without them.

He balanced and staggered and bullied across, and never fell until he was almost over—and that a startling quick slip of a fall that he saved from killing him by striking out to grip a broken-top rock just downstream. And striking and gripping it, cut the heel of his left hand smartly. But he held himself that way, only down on one knee, until he found his strength again, and slowly managed to stand against the river's buffeting.

"I name this fucking little river *The Stink*," Lee said after he was standing again, the sound of his voice wiped away by the river's noise. He felt better for talking, even though he couldn't hear what was said. "Fucking little river . . ."

The other bank was home sweet home, and Lee settled for sitting for a minute on damp rock well above the current. The cat could wait. He loosed the keeper off the Bisley Colt's, though, as he sat there, and used his wet bandana to wipe wet from the revolver. Have to clean this piece, the rifle, all his steel to a fare-thee-well as soon as he could manage, else they'd rust to pieces in this climate. Get some oil on them.

He got his breath, and, with the revolver still in his hand, climbed up to where the jaguar lay.

It had fallen back down from that higher ledge it had attempted, dying, and lay on its side as if it had galloped into death. Its eyes were almost closed, narrowed, deep-lashed. It looked to be staring out back over the river, as if still trying to make out what sort of wasp or hornet or wild bee had come flying to sting it so, with such a noise, to make it die.

The beast's tongue was spilling out from the side of its jaw; it lay wonderfully still and seemed quite dead, but Lee shouted to be sure—realized the shout was gone into the river's sounds, bent and found a shard of stone and threw it to strike the jaguar at its side.

No movement.

Lee walked the last few feet, knelt, and put his hurt left hand on the jaguar's flank. It felt like warm beaver fur over India rubber over oak. A wonderful sort of a thing to feel.

Lee took the left foreleg—as hard and dense and big around as the fat end of a baseball bat—and levered the limp beast over.

It was a female. She'd been shot just those fresh three times—the right shoulder, and two into her back. Soft, small pink teats were almost hidden in her belly's creamy fur. Likely had kittens denned somewhere above and had surely not been hunting on Stirrup, surely not been shot at and hit the night before.

That was another beast. Still roaming, now, injured and furious—or dying, fly-blown in some tangle, puzzled.

Nimrod.

When a man stopped hunting, except for food, he should stay stopped. Or certain sure, he'd make a fool of himself, and do no animals favors.

He'd have to lie to the men, of course—say it was this female all along had downed the beeves. Say he'd done the job in fine style. Or better, let *them* say it, and preserve the *Patron's* silence. His dignity.

Getting back over was even more difficult.

Lee had wrapped his cut hand in his bandanna but there was little he could do about the blood dripping from the jaguar's hide draped over his shoulders. He could only hope it was true that piranhas didn't care for swift water.

The cub didn't help, either, mewing for milk in the crook of an arm and putting a considerable set of claws into Lee's shoulder whenever the water knocked him staggering. Lee could only be grateful the big cat had had just the one— though that one, an old child, appeared mighty spoiled, mighty touchy. No great pleasure in getting the babe out of its mother's den, either. Hadn't cared for Lee at all—had yowled for Mama, scratched like fury, and done its damndest to bite Lee's nose clear off. And all this at less than a pound in weight, and its eyes barely open.

What was to be done with the little terror, God only knew. Lee supposed the gaucho's children would be pleased enough to be bitten and scratched while roaring around the *estancia* with the kitten, at least until the beast grew larger. Then, likely, the cub would have to be caged and hauled deep into the *Mato* to be released.

It would all be trouble and a chore and Lee likely wouldn't have considered it, but that the mother cat had been so beautiful a beast . . . killed in error.

As it was, he was happy enough only getting back across the Slick—cub, pelt, sore hand and all. Not as happy, though, as the dun to see him after no doubt considering itself abandoned. The small horse whinnied, cavorted, butted Lee with his nose, paying no heed whatsoever to the jaguar cub, or the jaguar pelt—and acting, all in all, more like a dog than a horse. Hadn't cared, apparently, for the notion of staying forever tied to a tree in the *Mato Grosso*.

It took a time to settle the cub in a saddle-bag. The dun might not have had objection to a young *tigre,* but the *tigre* absolutely had objection to the horse. Hard to believe the little son-of-a-bitch could do man that much damage with milk teeth.

FIVE

"Oh, ho . . . *oh, ho!*" Arturo was very pleased, pleased with the pelt, pleased with the cub. It was just the sort of nonsense that *Patrons* would get up to, given half a chance.

The gauchos and their people had gathered round when Lee rode in at sunset on a tired horse with a hungry kitten. Nacio had taken care of the horse, the children had carried the jaguar cub off to suckle it at an unlucky she-goat's tit, and Lee had left the gauchos and their women fingering the raw pelt to walk past the arbor (he had yet to see an edible grape hanging off of it) and up the steps into his shack.

He was damned glad to be home.

Glad enough to see Bonifacia ready with a tin mug of coffee for him, a platter of *asado:* capybara, goat meat, murderous sausages, and—wonder of wonders—a few chunks of beef.

He'd stood to eat his dinner; his hind end was too saddle-sore for sitting. Then, though it was far from full dark, had set the empty platter down, walked to his fine, big bed, sat, tugged his boots off, rolled onto the coverlet, a flat quilt Bonifacia had sewn from squares of rag, grumbling about the work all the while—and fell into sleep like a stone.

Dreamed that night for sure. Dreamed of spotted cats in spotted forests. One of the cats that also flew talked with Lee at great length in that dream. Talked with him about deep-earth mining, of all things. Copper mining. Talked about the squared-timber shore, its uses in resisting pressure from all points in a working. *"Revolutionary,"* the spotted cat said, eating a sweet potato, skin and all. *"Revolutionary."*

Lee agreed, afraid that if he didn't, the cat wouldn't lead him out of the Mato. As it turned out, however, the cat didn't have to do so—the Indian girl, Corazon, waked him sliding under the covers. Sent by Bonifacia, no doubt, to keep him company. Lee often saw the old woman's shadow at the kitchen walkway, the few hours he spent at home. Watching him, listening . . .

Other ranchers would have beaten the old lady for spying or fired her off the place. Lee didn't trouble. She was company, lurking there, and he'd never heard of a beating taking the twist out of a human heart. If the old woman wanted to play Mama, let her.

Half awake, he turned in bed to Corazon, to hug the big-bellied girl to him . . . smell the woman odor rising from her like the smell of freshed back bread. And back to sleep . . . back to sleep, diving into it as a man might into a stock tank of warm water, for ease and for refreshment.

* * *

Arturo had done very well with his two days. He'd seen to it the men had put in a half-mile of good tight fencing from the road north of the river, where Lee's grazing marched with Orellana's. Not that Lee had had trouble with Philipe Orelanna, but the stretch of sweet grass there, superior to the bunch and river grass that grew further west, was the sort of grass that men might fight over if they had good cause to fight.

Lee thought the fencing a sensible step, and had laid the fence a good fifty feet on his side of the property line. Arturo had said the Orellana men had ridden to the place to watch the fencing going up but had made no move to hinder it.

Had put the stretch of fencing in, had earmarked the healthy herd and separated calves, had tacked railing up where the stud had kicked it loose from the south side of the house corral, and had at least made a start (though not much of a start) on trenching the slope behind the out-house backing the gaucho's lean-to's. That place had been a place of severe stinks for some time now, and Lee, to his men's surprise, had determined to do something about it. Namely, to trench the down-slope out and line those trenches with busted roof tiles which had been purchased cheap at Tucuman.

This undertaking Arturo had only commenced with some half-hearted shovel scratchings, some unsteady stick markers stuck at intervals into the ground.

"We'll do better than that, by God," Lee said, examining the site upon the morning after his return. Arturo and a gaucho named Placido (who was, as it happened, far from being any such thing) stood by, mournfully observing the scratched slope, the great heap of broken tiles.

"I was not born to dig shit-holes." Placido, speaking with heat, but without anger.

"You will by God dig this one, or pack your nonsense off of my land! A gaucho can't be forever on his horse. Occasionally, it is necessary to pick up a shovel!" Lee in reply—with heat, without anger. These men were, in fact, wonderful stock handlers for all they didn't understand the use of a good length of rope, but, alas, mightly slack concerning work afoot. Credit to Arturo he'd got that line of fencing in. About all they were eager to do afoot was to fight, fuck, eat, and jump up and down on a throat-cut steer to bleed it out for an *asado* barbecue, preparatory to more eating.

Placido, with five small children to feed, and a reputation for violence which would have kept many *estancieros* from hiring him on, subsided at Lee's reply, only hawking and spitting off to the side.

"Get Carlos, Papo, and Chucho to help you—have them trench these hen-scratchings deep enough to stand in to their chests. When those are complete, call me. We'll have the *Indios* (old Martin, old Louis) lay the tiles along them. Then, here on the Stirrup, we will have the finest shit-house, and the best drained, in the whole of the *Chaco*. Down in the pampas, I'm told, those sheep-herders that call themselves gauchos crap onto the ground like their sheep. Those people know nothing of style.''

That went down well however it traduced the men who rode the great grasslands to the south, and Arturo and Placido nodded firm agreement.

Odd, how wonderfully different men might be when they had, after all, the same ways to make their livings. In Idaho Territory, at Spade Bit, Lee would have had only to ride to an out-house slope with some men, look down at the dirt, say "Trench it," and ride away.

Down here, though, more of a song-and-dance seemed required. Perhaps because of the language, Spanish being so much more formal. Perhaps these men's half-Indian hearts required more soothing for their shames, the sufferings of their mothers and grandmothers . . .

There was this out-house drain . . . And more fencing—not the Orellana stretch, this time; a rancher could take only so much fencing from accustomed grass, whatever the rights of the matter. Lee might fence his pastures along the river, use those meadows as larger holding pens that the corrals or rope cow-folds. It would mean less fussing and chivvying with the stock, less driving of them. Better for the animals, no doubt about it.

Drain . . . and the fencing. Might do to go into Tucuman for more of the broken tiles—use them as drain-stuff alongside the bañandos, perhaps keep those wets in grass and cotton for three seasons, instead of two.

Would be too much digging for the gauchos,

though. Have to bring in mestizo labor from the villages around Sante Fe. That trash would dig for a peso tenth a day. Drain every soak he had on Stirrup . . . Make their eyes pop at the Kit Kat Club in Sante Fe.

Could all be done—should all be done.

Given time—and money.

A month and more later, the hottest weather beginning to ease off the slightest bit, a man named Enrique Portero, a small, dark brown fellow, a trash farmer just over the line of the land belonging to Gaspar Nuñoz (this land almost two day's ride up the Paraña) was discovered in his mean clearing, murdered by Indians. Portero had been lucky, since Cuchillo's men (no doubt it was Benudos) had apparently been hurried in disposing of him. The *Indios* had had more leisure in dealing with Portero's woman and four children. They had put this leisure to painstaking use, skinning that woman and her children alive, then throwing them into the coals of a large fire.

Lee heard this news while he and five men were working the remuda south, out of pasture too wet, however rich with grass, for the animal's hooves.

The gaucho who brought it, one of Nuñoz's men, was mighty excited at the prospect of *Indio* hunting. Truth was, he likely considered the sacrifice of Portero's family to have been well worth it, if it proved to mean a week or two off work while campaigning along the edges of the Chaco.

Bad news for Lee, though. Indian fighting was

well enough if you weren't one of the unlucky ones who took an arrow—was well enough, unless you had better things to do. And Lee had better things to do. *Chaco* ranchers were not easily let slide, not even for a week or two. The jungle came in too quickly . . . the jungle; *mestizo* nesters or other, cleverer men. It would take an extra week of work just to come even if he led most of his men off redskin chasing, but damned if he could see how to avoid it. No question this little matter of the Porteros was only the opening gun as far as Cuchillo was concerned. The Benudos, like all the *Chaco* tribes, were being driven to the wall as certainly as any tribes had been on the great American plans—though, from what Lee had read in the American papers freighted in every few months from the Capital, a few of the American tribes, some Comanches, some of the Northwest tribes, were still making trouble.

Only the opening gun. Cuchillo would have more ambutious notions than butchering some few no-accounts like the Porteros. He had, it was true, a great ally in the endless forest from which to raid as he chose, as long as he and his men weren't caught in the open in daylight by the *estancieros* and their gaucho horsemen. But the Sioux and Cheyenne had also considered the distance and depth of country to be their fortress. Gold-hunters and farmers had shown those tribes their error. Lee supposed it would be lumbermen who would break the fastness of the *Chaco,* given time.

Cuchillo would know all this, and know it

without reading newspapers.

The Porteros were an opening gun. Considering the matter, Lee wished to heaven he had let the Indian go, the one that had planted the arrow in Pico Rosas' back. Fellow must have been an important man, perhaps a wizard of some sort, a man whose death Cuchillo could not allow to let pass unavenged. Spirits might have come flying to the chief in his dreams—a monkey eagle, perhaps, clacking its beak . . .

No white man understood Indian lives, that was certain.

Not their lives, perhaps, but a man could damn well understand their methods of war. The Porteros had been struck by a large party of men, not two or three wandering warriors out to butcher stock. Planned, then. And if planned, then planned with a purpose. To draw the guachos north . . . ?

It seemed likely, especially since the Javanches lived just north of Gaspar Nuñoz' land, and those Indians (what was left of the tribe) were no friends to Benudos.

A nice puzzle, figuring Cuchillo's main line of attack.

Something to mull over on the ride to Juan Soto's *cantina e merchandencia*. He would have to take both Arturo and Fat Nacio on this ride—a gaucho could be left out of only so much—and a formidable gaucho certainly not left out of a meeting of *Patrons* at Juan Soto's, denied a chance to swagger about the yard telling lies and drinking raw rum, a chance to sit around a good fire telling lies and slicing bites of asado beef off at their lips as they chewed at strips of the leathery, hot-sauced stuff, the long, razor-edged knife blades flickering a fraction from the tips of their noses.

No denying Arturo and Fat Nacio those pleasures; they'd pout nad sulk like children for a month and do damn little work.

He'd have to leave the Paraguayan in charge—a young man named Pedro Rey, round-faced as a pumpkin though thin in the body, and so short as to be almost a dwarf. This Pedro was as near full-blooded *Indio* as any gaucho would admit to being, and no doubt was an Argentina because the authorities in Asunçion wished to hang him. Still, the other men respected him. Most, Lee supposed, feared him. And he was a willing worker and fine all 'round hand, though with a peculiarity of silence. Lee had never heard the young man say a word. Nods, smiles, head-shakes and frowns seemed to suit him all the way.

So when Nuñoz' man had galloped off, full of news, toward McGee's headquarters fifteen miles away, having left it up to Lee to attend or not the meeting at Soto's the next day, Lee cursed, spit his cigar stub onto the ground by the dun's left fore hoof, whistled his men from their herding, and told them of the Porteros' sorry finish, of Arturo and Fat Nacio's election to accompany him to the meeting of *Patrons* and of Pedro Rey's appointment as *Jefe* in their absence.

That had all gone down well enough, with the promise that a great campaign, if put in train, would require many more men to come riding to join him.

Went down well enough and Lee set the Paraguayan to the chores that must be done, grim at the notion of that jolly campaign and the harm it would do Stirrup by slipshod and absence, let alone by Indian raids and fire-arrows.

Set the Paraguayan on, spoke very firmly to the men—and jackass who rode out after him to Soto's without being sent for would collect a boot up his asshole—then gave them permission to butcher a beef (they would have done so anyway, likely, once he was a day or so gone) made an obscene gesture of farewell, and rode off with his two Myrmidons on the trail down to Orellana's line, a few miles further, Juan Soto's *cantina* and *merchandencia*.

Juan McGee and his *jefe,* Miguel Cesarpiña, a withered, wire-muscled old man with a face like a raisin, caught up with Lee late in the afternoon. They'd ridden through a stretch of swamp to cut their ride a little shorter, and their horses' legs and bellies were caked with dark red drying mud.

The five of them rode together down the south bank of the Paraña. None of them with much to say . . . McGee a few remarks on Portero, whom he had met a time or two in Sante Fe. "Nothing much to the little fellow," McGee said. "Not a bad sort, for a clearing-man."

"The wife was a whore," old Cesarpiña said, old enough and tough enough to say what he pleased when he pleased. Cesarpiña was a very good Catholic. "A bitch whore, who undoubtedly

received the punishment of Our Lord at the hands
of those savages.''

Silence, after that, for quite a while.

The Paraña, never a very deep river, though a
rifle-shot and more across, flowed smooth and
easy down this stretch of country, red-brown,
untroubled by any rapids, any straits. Rumored to
be *piranha* in it, in the slow eddies along both sides
of the shore. These rumors were enough to keep
the ranchers crossing their cattle way downstream
near Soto's. The water was moving faster there,
rougher over shelves of grey pebbles, an
occasional rounded stone; and there was sink-
holes, a few of them deep enough to drown any
steer that floundered into them.

These losses the *estancieros* gladly excepted
rather than chance seeing half a herd eaten alive
while they staggered in a foaming welter of red-
dyed water, of occasional, silver-flashing fish
bodies as the piranha leaped up out of the red-
crimson spray, clung for an instant to the flank of
some moaning beef, then fell back into the water,
leaving a neat baseball-sized wound spurting
bright blood.

Lee crossed his cattle in fast water just as all the
other ranchers did and for much the same reasons
—the horror of those possible deaths as much as
the money loss involved.

Here, then, and for many miles more, the river
ran undisturbed by any cattle, any horseman. All
on account of possible shoals and schools of
small, silvery, fat fish.

"I don't care what the woman had been,''

McGee, after a smile and more of silent riding. His gaucho's remarks apparently were still troubling him. "I won't believe that God would author such a horror as that. The work of the devil is what I would call it!"

Lee glanced across McGee's front and saw Cesarpiña's ancient eyes, dull-brown and dangerous, as the old man glanced at his *Patron*.

Hard to think of anything more foolish than to argue on religion with a primitive. Lee'd got a whiff of McGee's breath as he spoke; sad fellow was drunk.

And nothing more spoken of, religion or anything else, until Lee said something (as with twilight, they rode into view of Soto's) about the Portero raid having been a ruse, and only the beginning of trouble. Cesarpiña had nodded at that but said nothing. McGee hadn't seemed to hear.

SIX

The *estancieros* were there, their fine horses tied to the long rail at the side of Soto's shed. Klinger's sorrel stud—too much horse for him, as it happened; Orellana's mare; Gaspar Nuñoz' *Andaluz;* Alphonso Gutierrez' black, a light-stepping animal with one blue eye. Raimundo Jaurez' horse . . . Mendez' horse. Two or three animals Lee didn't know.

The *Patrons* in Soto's—their men in the grove along the river. Here, in fading light, the gauchos had slung their hammocks from the saplings, stacked their carbines, and lounged now around a large fire fed with driftwood collected at the bank of the river. One was playing a tango on his guitar for a gaucho and one of Soto's Indian whores to dance to. They were dancing it very well. Other men were getting up to dance with this or that young whore or, failing to find a more appropriate partner, dancing with each other through the sinuous turning figures, the slow sliding steps, first this way, then that.

Creased, weather-tanned faces, broken-knuckled hands. Soft, baggy trousers cinched with broad belts (small pistols, long knives, silver *maté* straws in those broad belts). Soft-top boots. Soft Spanish and, occasionally Indian words spoken. And, on a wide rusty iron grill over seething coals, a collection of forest meats—parrot, capybara, monkey—some slabs of beef, and crude, fat blood sausages, all sizzling, spattering under red running sauce. The rich, acrid, oily smell of the *asado* drifting through the saplings on the fire's smoke.

The first dancer was very fine—had, Lee supposed, been to the Capital at some time, to learn such steps. The Indian girl was drunk, or drugged with some forest concoction, and couldn't keep pace with the man, but the gaucho danced for them both. Danced with the guitar, really.

Lee nodded Arturo and Fat Nacio over to join the others, and Cesarpiño reined his horse after them without waiting for McGee's say-so one way or the other.

Lee and the Irishman tied their mounts to the long rail and walked up the steps. Soto had his shed on stilts, a concession to the whims of the Paraña in flood. Through a wire-screened door (the first such that Lee had ever seen, tremendous novelty, and the severely defended apple of Soto's eye) and on into the saloon side of the store.

Here, a long plank bar resting on a dozen rum barrels in a row ran down the right hand wall, stacks of dirty bottles and dirtier glasses on the shelves behind it. Tables and chairs on the corridor of flooring flanking the partition separated the bar from Soto's dry-goods, scales, knickknacks, flour, corn meal, cottonseed oil, dried caiman hides, rolls of German barbed wire, and so forth and so forth.

The place had the smell common to such establishments. It stank of spilled rum and vomit, faintly of urine, of coal-oil, canvas, gun-oil, paint, sugar candy, salt pork, *yerba maté,* and cheap perfume.

It smelled of everything. It was full of yellow lamplight.

The *estancieros* were standing at the bar, sitting at tables, some with cousins or brothers—men of their own families, men they could trust if it came to an Indian fight . . . men, perhaps, they could not trust well enough to leave at home with their stock or their wives. The ranchers greeted Lee pleasantly enough, McGee with some reserve.

They were an odd-looking lot, these lords of the *Gran Chaco,* and not all Spanish sorts by any means. Klinger was there, of course, though he happened to be dark enough to pass for an Indian himself. There was an Englishman named Robert Belter, whose horse Lee hadn't noticed at the rail. Belter was a large, fair, tough-looking man, with two fingers missing off his left hand. Lee had met Belter only once before, when the Englishman had gotten drunk at the Kit Kat Club and demonstrated his strength by lifting a spinet piano a foot off the floor and holding it there while Alphonso Gutierrez, reaching high, poured a shaker of *Daquaries* into Belter's mouth. This was impressive enough to convince Lee that the Englishman was no-one to bear-wrestle in a fight.

One thing, however, all these desperate men had in common—a look of extreme stubbornness, a sort of battered obstinacy. Truculence.

There were few of them who had not murdered or stolen to achieve their great properties. And those pacific and lucky few had instead performed prodigies of back-breaking work over many, many years in conditions fit to kill most men who only visited.

They were, in sum, an impressive crew. Lee had seen no harder faces among the great ranchers of the Rockies. These, like those, were men well used to being laws unto themselves. And more than sufficient law, at that.

Now they were met to consider the Indian *Jefe,* Cuchillo—and fierce as that red-man might be, and secure in his palace of endless green, Lee would not have bet a five-dollar piece on his chances against these men in the long run.

In the short run, however, matters would likely run some little bit rough.

Jorge Cevellos, a presumed junior partner of Soto's, was tending bar for him while the cadaverous senior partner (thin as a rail, his hair plastered flat in extravagant spit-curls) had ventured to join his betters in Pisco sours and rum punches. Lee asked Cevellos for a rum and guava juice, a drink he had become fond of, and stood beside McGee at the plank bar, the Irishman having ordered up a large rum of his own, and already sipping at it.

The affair appeared to have some of the aspects of a party about it—unusual for all these movers-

and-shakers of the territory to be gathered together. A meeting, no doubt, that brought to mind old triumphs, failures, grudges, feuds . . .

A few murders as well, likely.

Still, a generally festive air prevailed. These were men of continuous effort, of grinding toil and perfect and constant alertness for any danger, any difficulty. This meeting, therefore, though serious in intent, represented a sort of holiday— marauding Indians seeming, however immediate a threat, rather minor and romantic compared with land thieves, cattle diseases, and the failure of various banks in the Captital.

There was also, among themselves, an opportunity for business to be done, and these men went about that in a relaxed, merry sort of way, talking bulls and hectares, lumbering and cotton; the difficulties of the current price of silver, gross incompetence at the Capital, the necessity of General Roca's taking some sort of a hand in running the country.

"Bad luck at the show, Morgan." Alphonso Gutierrez, ordinarily not a friendly man, smiling in a companionable way. Referring to the cattle show where Lee's bull had won only the red.

"The Italian—" Lee started to say, not hesitating to blame the judge for that miscarriage of justice.

"Yes, I've heard of that *cabron*. Rizzio—a professor in the line of cattle breeding, I understand."

"Bred to an asshole, himself," Lee said, still mighty warm over that theft of the blue ribbon.

"You should have seen the camel he gave the blue to. The fucking thing had five legs!"

"The wop judge?" Belter, the big Englishman, a clay jug of Pisco sour overwhelmed in his three-fingered hand. "That piece of human shit is in the pay of the *pampanieros*. We won't get good judging until we run out our own show up here. A *Chaco* show! 'Til then, Morgan, we can expect to get royally screwed, whatever animals we enter."

Hard to say that was wrong, so Lee agreed with it. McGee, by his side, grunted, and said something about the Porteros, and a massacre being of some slightly greater importance than ribbons at a stock show. This was so odd a remark that Lee could hardly think of something to say to pass over it, and both Belter and Alphonso Gutierrez appeared astonished, then embarrassed, then quickly changed the subject to the zinc coating of the new German barbed wire which hopefully would keep that fencing material from rusting to powder after two or three years of use.

"Four years," Lee said. "That coating will give us four years. If those idiots from Farben would cross the ocean to see where we're using their fucking wire, they might bring themselves to galvanize it with something tougher than *weiner schnitzel!*"

"An insult!" Klinger called from down the room.

"The truth!" Lee said. "And Glidden could do worse than ship some good stuff down here."

"Yankee nonsense!" called Klinger, and made an obscene gesture.

"They use thorn fencing in Africa," Belter said.

"Not here, please God," Gutierrez said. "We'd

have nothing *but* thorn, from border to border, in six months. If you bring in thorn, Belter, it'll be war, I warn you."

"No, no, wouldn't work here, I agree. Too damn much rain—you'd never keep control of the stuff. And it's a shame. Works damn well in Africa. East Africa, anyway."

"And what's the rainfall in East Africa?"

"All right, I agree. Much less rainfall . . ."

"Now," Gutierrez said, with a glance at Juan McGee, "that that's settled, and Señor Belter is not going to destroy my grazing, what the hell do we do about these Indians?"

"Kill the chief, you kill the tribe." Belter.

"For the time being, surely. But how do we kill Cuchillo when we can't find him?"

"He'll come out," Lee said. "He's getting ready to come out, now."

"Listen to that—the cowboy knows!" Klinger again, smiling. Klinger was a decent man, and well liked, not least because he was the nearest man who was also nearest to being a doctor.

"I think not," Gaspar Nuñoz said, very politely—and, being polite, got up from the table where he and Klinger had been talking and walked over to speak with Lee directly.

"It seems to me, though of course I may be mistaken, that this Portero affair is only the first of similar little *razzias* that may occur from time to time. Nothing of great importance . . . unlikely to be very damaging, and very unlikely to occur where we might bring our men against them in force."

Nuñoz was a very handsome young man—sandy haired, grey-eyed as a Scot. A son of one of the old Spanish families from the northern provinces, Asturias and such. Nuñoz had been in the Chaco now for some seven years, having killed a man in a duel over some opera dancer when he was eighteen years old. This, to be sure, had not been enough to exile him from Buenos Aires, his family being very important. The exile had occured three years later when, in another duel (with a furious husband) Nuñoz had again proved too good a shot. The husand had also belonged to an important family, with the result that Gaspar Nuñoz had been sent into exile in the provinces where, to the apparent surprise of all, he'd proved a hard-working, even brutally efficient rancher who had in various ways managed to become very rich, very successful.

He had had to kill only three more men in exile.

"I propose we treat mosquito bites as they deserve—until the opportunity arises to swat the mosquito."

"Very fine," McGee said, lifting his head from his rum. "Very fine. And how many Señora Porteros are these 'mosquitos' to be allowed to skin, to save you and your men some additional time and work, some additional money?"

Nuñoz looked surprised at this.

"One regrets, of course," he said, "but—"

"*One regrets,*" McGee said, and put his rum glass down on the bark planking with a snap. "And I say that if we swagger about here as the lords of creation and grind these poor farmers' faces in the dirt, then we are less than men if we fail them when trouble comes! I say any man would let a woman's murder . . . let a man's wife die such a death . . . Only a coward would allow such a thing to pass and do nothing about it but save his money!''

Lee felt that McGee, drunk, was speaking more in confusion of his own wife's fearful death than that of the Portero woman. Though, that he had an argument concerning the *estancieros'* responsibility was difficult enough to deny. Certainly hadn't meant it as an insult to Nuñoz, or any of the rest of them.

''Surely,'' Gaspar Nuñoz said, his fine grey eyes cold as dirty snow, ''surely that remark was not intended for me personally.''

''Of course not,'' Lee said, and would have gone on to argue with McGee himself, but Nuñoz held up a fine, sun-browned long-fingered hand to stop him.

''A moment, Señor, if you please. That remark concerning cowardice, McGee—surely not intended for me, personally?''

There was that in Nuñoz' voice, which was not loud at all, that quieted the room as a gunshot might have done.

McGee, for his part, looked only baffled, dully angry. ''You are God-damned right it was,'' he said. ''Meant for you, and for any other cowardly son-of-a-bitch who allows women to be butchered to spare trouble and the expense of a fight.''

''Unfortunate,'' Nuñoz said, and looked genuinely sorry. ''Most unfortunate.''

"You damn fool," Belter to McGee. "Retract that—and *pronto!*"

"The hell I will," McGee said, and shoved his rum glass back out of his way with his elbow, allowing his hand to rest on the edge of the bar, just over the small pistol holstered at the side of his wide belt.

"Don't be a damn fool," Lee said. "Gaspar, he's drunk."

"I am not!"

"He's drunk."

Nuñoz turned on his heel and walked away from them, a dozen feet, perhaps, further down the bar. There he stopped, turned to face them, reached behind him, and rather slowly drew a long-barreled revolver from the back of his belt. Weapon looked to be a Smith & Wesson .38 caliber piece to Lee.

Nuñoz held the drawn revolver down alongside his right thigh, muzzle pointed at he floor.

No man in the room moved, even a bit.

"I would certainly prefer not to kill you, Señor McGee," Nuñoz said. "Please apologize to me at once."

"For Christ's sake, Juan," Lee said, "you're making a God-damned fool of yourself! Tell the man you're sorry!"

McGee, staring at Nuñoz, jaw set, breathing heavy as a bull's, said not a word.

It came to Lee in that instant that the Irishman wished to die—had wished it ever since his wife had gone. Wished it, and was pleased enough now that the time had come. And it occurred to Lee directly after that, and very quickly, that the Irish-man's wish would also be the fulfillment of Lee's own desires.

Forty thousand acres—and Sarita McGee.

He had only to step aside.

"Gaspar . . ."

Only had to step aside . . .

"Gaspar. Juan's not himself—he's drunk." What a fool, Lee thought, to be interfering in this way. What a fool . . . "I ask you as a personal favor, let this pass."

Nuñoz flicked a glance at Lee. No expression there to read.

"Juan *is* very drunk," said Alphonso Gutierrez.

"Not nearly drunk enough to speak what he has spoken," Nuñoz said. "Let us step outside, Irish-man."

"Gaspar . . ." Some man said.

McGee started to move, but Lee put out a hand and stopped him.

"Let it pass, Nuñoz," Lee said.

"Or you will interest yourself in this matter?" Nuñoz didn't seem disturbed by the notion.

"Leave me be!" McGee said and Lee, keeping his eyes on Nuñoz, shoved the Irishman back hard against the bar.

"Gentlemen—please . . ." Soto, and wasting his time.

" 'Greater love hath no man than this,' " Nuñoz said, smiling. Down the length of the bar, the *estancieros* leaned back and away on either side as if a great wind had come blowing down the room.

113

"Get away!" McGee said, and struck at Lee's restraining arm as Nuñoz raised his revolver very quickly and aimed it at Lee all in a single movement, and smoothly.

Lee, McGee wrestling at his left side, drew and shot Gaspar Nuñoz—but didn't kill him. The bullet struck Nuñoz low on his left side, so that he was off balance as he fired. That round snapped barely past Lee's head as he pulled away from McGee and shot at Nuñoz again. Didn't see if he'd hit him.

Men were shouting. Shouting.

Nuñoz was walking backward, obscure in powder smoke, his left hand at his side where Lee had hit him. Lifted his revolver again, took the same swift deliberate aim.

Lee and Nuñoz fired together, the sounds of the gunshots unbearable in the room. Lee saw the lance of flame from Nuñoz's pistol, heard a loud smacking sound, and saw in the same instant Gaspar Nuñoz's head suddenly split like a struck melon, broken from the cheek up into the forehead, so that an eye appeared in that wound, far out of place, until the blood sprayed to cover it as Nuñoz fell straight back and down. Hit the floor quite hard.

A dead man—and Lee with not a wound on him.

"Mother of God," said Alphonso Gutierrez, "but you are quick with that pistol!" The barroom was so quiet, so suddenly still, that Gutierrez' voice rang out like a shouting preacher's.

Lee turned to look at Gutierrez in some surprise

at having heard him, at having heard any talking, his ears were ringing so from the gun-shots.

They turned back further and saw the big Englishman, Belter, lying cursing against the bar, McGee just kneeling to see to him. Belter had a right shoulder running bright red, his canvas jacket soaked down the sleeve already.

Had caught one of Nuñoz' rounds. The first, Lee thought. The one that had snapped so neatly past his head.

What a surprise . . . come into Soto's for a meeting, and a drink or two—step in for a drunken Irishman who wanted no such help, and come to shooting with Nuñoz. Over nothing at all.

"Shot him three times . . ." Tall, stooped, Orellana, kneeling beside what was left of handsome, dangerous Gaspar Nuñoz. Orellana shaking his head, looking down the powder-smoky room at Lee as if Lee were some beast loose out of a menagerie. Looking as if Gaspar Nuñoz had not killed men, had not forced the fight, had not tried his best, shooting.

"The man insisted on trying me," Lee said, his voice sounding very odd to him. "And would have killed McGee, and McGee with no chance against him."

"Man, you are fast with that pistol!"

Lee was getting tired of Alphonso Gutierrez. Tired of his talking. He gave Gutierrez a hard look, and that fellow stopped talking.

Noises at the door. Gauchos curious at the shooting, crowding in to see.

"Oh, God damn! *God damn!*" A gaucho

named Silvero, one of Nuñoz' men. Silvero was squat as a sawn trunk. "Who is it has murdered my *Patron?*"

"Shut your mouth, man—and all of you, get out of here!" Orellana said, and raised his quirt to strike Silvero across the face, but the gaucho ducked away, and went to kneel beside Nuñoz. "Who is the dog who had done this?"

"Listen, you—" Orellana reached for the man's collar to drag him away. Klinger said something, strode to help him.

"Leave him!" Lee said, and saw Fat Nacio shove through the bunch at the door. Nacio had his revolver in his hand.

"You—Silvero," Lee said, and walked toward the man, toward what was left of Gaspar Nuñoz. "I shot your *Jefe*. He wished a fight and had his pistol in his hand, and fought like a brave man." Lee's voice wasn't sounding as strange to him as it had a moment before.

Great noise among the gauchos at the door, not wanting to be crushed between great stones rolling, not wanting, either, to be left out of a fight, or seem to be backward in protecting their own *Patrons*.

"All you men!" Klinger, shouting. "You get your asses out of here!"

"You, Silvero," Lee said, "ride to Señor McGee's *estancia,* get a wagon there, and come back here for your *Patron.*"

The stocky man knelt for a moment more, staring up at Lee.

"You heard the *Patron,*" a rancher named

116

Raimundo Juarez said. "Do as you've been told." Juarez was still standing at the bar, still had his drink in his hand. "Go on—get off your ass, man."

Slowly, Silvero climbed to his feet. He didn't look at Lee again, didn't look down at the ruins of Gaspar Nuñoz, either. Turned and pushed his way through the gauchos at the door. Fat Nacio winked at Lee as the other man went past him. Then Nacio put his pistol back into his belt, turned and started out, herding the other gauchos in front of him, calling them old ladies who'd never heard gunfire before.

With the gauchos out of the place, except for a few curious faces peering at the edges of the door and the sills of the windows along the building's side, Soto's seemed perfectly still, perfectly quiet.

Two or three of the *estancieros* looked at Lee (the others avoided looking at him) and Lee realized he still held the Bisley Colt's in his hand, like some drunken kid stunned by his first fight. He reloaded the weapon while they watched him, then he holstered it.

"This is a grave matter," Orellana said—to himself, it appeared. By which Lee assumed he meant that a gentleman, and a rich gentleman at that, had just had half his head blown away. And by, Lee thought, some mighty poor shooting, though it had impressed men not used to fine, fast revolver work. Were he to start making gunplay of this sort a habit, it would be wise to practice. If Nuñoz had not been so almighty careful of his aim, so formal in the matter, he would certainly have put at least one hole in the cowboy opposing him.

The whole thing being so damned foolish . . .

So damned foolish. Disgusting, might be a better word for it.

"Not such a grave matter," Lee said. "More a stupid and disgusting matter."

No one had anything to say to that—nor did anyone ask Cevellos for another Pisco or straight rum, either. Gaspar Nuñoz, who had bled a small red lake from his ripped head, seemed to attract all possible sound to himself and smother it before it was made.

"I suppose," Klinger finally said, "we should have our meeting in the store."

Seconded. Except for Juan McGee, who walked slowly out the front door, and was gone.

While Klinger stayed behind to tend to the punctured Englishman—who from the steady rumble of cursing did not seem liable to die— the other men and Lee filed to the partition door-way and through it, into the *merchandencia,* to talk about Benudo Indians amidst bolts of cotton cloth, kegs of nails and iron screw-bolts, leaving Soto behind to delicately approach the little lake of blood with a mop—work that somehow seemed inappropriate for Cevellos or the Indian girls to do. Too near Nuñoz' ruined head.

SEVEN

"Post patrols along the river—follow the *Indios* as they sneak past. . ."

"If you *see* them sneaking past!"

"Post patrols, then follow them in. Catch those red dogs in the open—watch what happens when our fellows catch those dogs in the open!"

"Holy Mary and Her Saints!" Enrique Mendez, a plump man (rumored to have intercourse with his own sister, Doña Eustacia, who was the only female on his *rancho*, bar a few half-witted talatu women who did their laundry). This and other crimes were attributed to Enrique Mendez, but not to his face, since men who angered this little fat one, even dangerous men, often vanished thereafter quite suddenly, (perhaps on their way to a stock sale, or a visit to a neighbor), and were never seen again.

Mendez was a very quiet man, very plump, a notoriously poor horseman. Pleasant, even pleading brown eyes. His sister, also, was nothing much to look at. Except for those odd disappearings, in fact—seven or eight of them in the last few years—Mendez, for all his money, would barely have been treated with respect.

As things stood, however, he was.

"Holy Mary and Her Saints!" he said. "Call Cortez and his cavalry into it if you wish to be campaigning all over our range. If you want our cotton trampled by soldiers, by drunken gauchos! I, for one, want no such thing!"

Mendez was the only one of the ranchers—except perhaps Klinger—who treated Lee precisely as they had before the shooting. The other men, still able to smell the gunsmoke from the saloon side of the shed, able to hear the swish of Soto's mop, either deferred to Lee in small and subtle ways, or grew harsher with him, more prickly, so that he wouldn't believe them afraid.

Lee had no illusions of this awkwardness being permanent. It was an affair of the hour, of the next few days at most. Then it would be history and treated as history. Then, the other *estancieros* would be once more at ease with him. Now, the freshness of the thing had unsettled them.

"For Christ's sake, the Army is no use up here!" Man named Samoza. Lee knew very little of him; supposed to have considerable property north of Nuñoz' place. And in fact, might now owe Lee a great deal. There would be little to prevent a neighbor from shifting boundaries now that Gaspar was dead. Nuñoz must have been a rather uncomfortable neighbor in any case. Samoza was likely very glad to be hearing the swish of Soto's mop next door.

"I think," Lee said, noticing a gratifying degree of attention (nothing like a killing to turn up the lamp), "I think that Cuchillo knows all this as well as we do. Maybe better. Why, then, not surprise him? Do something he *doesn't* expect?"

"Such as?" said plump Mendez.

"Such as climbing off our fine horses, taking food, canteens, rifles and compasses and going into the *Mato* after him."

The ranchers looked at Lee as if killing one of his own had just proved a symptom of general madness.

"Go into the *Mato? Hombre,* that would be meeting the savage on his own ground!" Raimundo Juarez, sitting on a nail keg across the room, shook his head.

"And why not?" Lee said. "Cuchillo seems willing enough to meet us on *our* ground! I don't mean that we should go as a mob and attempt to surprise the Indians in their village, kill a hundred or so. We couldn't do that, anyway. But we can go into the *Mato;* compasses would keep us oriented to the river, keep us from being lost. We could raid in there, kill a few of them every time we go in . . ."

"And lose some of our own men!"

"You can't beat Cuchillo on the cheap," Lee said, careful to keep his temper. "It will cost you something."

"That's true enough," Mendez said. "But to go into the *Mato* after these savages . . ." He pursed plump lips, considering it. "It seems an unlikely prospect."

"Listen," Lee said. "We can afford losses better than Cuchillo can. If he loses more than a few warriors, his people will believe that bad medicine. He'll have to move deeper into the jungle, further back from the Paraña. But his people need a river—for water, for the fishing. He'll have to move all the way back to the *Ururape,* and that is forty miles into the *Mato.* Way too far for him to raid us.''

"There's some sense to that," Orellana said. The gentlemen was leaning against one of the roof posts, smoking a cheroot. Seemed to Lee that Orellana was beginning to get over his mad about the shooting. Handsome Gaspar, so freshly slaughtered, was already becoming history. He was gone, however recently. Cuchillo was not.

"Some sense to that," Orellana said.

"More sense to poison that red dog if we can get him to an asado. Perhaps Cortez will come with his cavalry, promise the Benudos a peace conference. We could give those animals enough rat-poison to solve the problem in a night!'' This from Samoza, an elderly man in a fine grey suit, Oxford shoes. Samoza was a Paraguayan—they'd had considerable success with poisoning Indians at peace parties, though, to be fair, their government disapproved of it.

"You're talking about a *Jefe,* and no fool," Raimundo Juarez said. "He'll take no poison from any white man.''

"Let us make at least a first decision now," Orellana said. "Let us do this—if the Benudos raid once more across the river (and we will now patrol to attempt to stop them)—if they cross once more and destroy our property, kill people, then we adopt *Señor* Morgan's suggestion, form small parties of well-armed men, and bring the fighting into the *Mato*."

"I don't look forward to that," Mendez said, "whatever you fire-eaters say."

Lee's mouth was feeling dry. He would have been very pleased with a rum and guava juice. Would have been even more pleased if that drink could have contained a little sliver of ice from the mountains.

"I don't look forward to that, either," he said. "It will be a bad business—only not quite so bad as being raided for the next several years, have people under our protection butchered, have our cattle and horses maimed. It's time, and past time, for these Indians to go back deeper into their forests."

"Settled then," Orellana said, and none of the *estancieros* disagreed. "We patrol our properties —send riders along the river, day and night. If Cuchillo gets through, sends a large band through again, despite our patrols, we will go across the river after them."

Mendez sighed, but no one said anything.

"Settled, then," Orellana said.

"What's settled? We're campaigning, are we?" Klinger strolled through the partition door.

"Belter?" Gutierrez said.

"Snoring like an infant," Klinger said. He had a glass of rum in his hand, raised it. "Mother's milk has sent our Englishman into the land of dreams. Shot through and through the right shoulder—cleared the top of the lung by not much, but just enough. The English are difficult to kill, particularly by accident.''

Klinger sat down on a coffee bag beside Lee, gave him a swift look and held out the rum glass.

"No, thanks.''

The ranchers were up now, well enough satisfied with their meeting. A few of them wandered back into the saloon, pleased to see the floor mopped, Nuñoz no longer stretched on the planking in his fine English riding boots, his once white, tailored shirt . . . his ruined head.

"In the back," Klinger said to Lee. "Our aristo duellist is in the saloon store room, waiting for his wagon." Klinger had never cared for Gaspar Nuñoz. "And if the wagon doesn't come fairly swiftly, our Gaspar will be considerably spoiled. The heat." Hadn't cared for him at all, apparently.

"Here—have a drink of this," Klinger said, and handed Lee the rum. "I must say I've always thought all that American wild west stuff considerably overdrawn—after all, the *Chaco* is not a kindergarten. Still, after seeing you shoot Nuñoz to pieces in there (I believe the whole affair took three or four seconds) I've had second thoughts. As, I'm certain, Nuñoz did as well. Too late." Klinger smiled and patted Lee on the shoulder. "Now, drink up that rum. It strikes me that you are not quite so tough a pastry as you would have the world believe."

Lee drank the rum down. "I've never taken any killing lightly, Carl."

" 'Any killing,' " Klinger said, and heaved

himself up off the coffee sack. "A pregnant phrase . . ." He stood looking down at Lee for a moment. "You Americans are very odd," he said, then shrugged. "Come back into the saloon now and let us see about getting you drunk. It would reassure the others to see you properly drunk."

The others had been thoroughly reassured.

Lee had ridden the long ride back to Stirrup—Arturo and Fat Nacio trailing behind, likewise drunk—in a haze of rum. To be sure, the rum had not kept his hands from trembling on his saddle-bow as he rode. Part of getting older, he supposed; killings appeared to take more out of him . . . made his hands shake. Made him feel ill sometimes. God knew Gaspar Nuñoz meant nothing to him—except as a possible rival for Sarita McGee, if it came to that . . .

Would have had her, too, if he'd kept his mouth out of that quarrel. Juan McGee had been looking for death; Nuñoz had been ready (for more reason than offended pride) to supply it. Must have noticed McGee's slide . . . must have thought as Lee had of the possibilities in that.

Stupid . . . stupid to have interfered. Had only to do nothing, for McGee to have been shot dead right there. Nuñoz could have been dealt with later.

Damned if he knew why that last round had struck so high. It was true that in a fight the bullet strikes tended to climb—recoil of the piece—and fearful men held their heads high and back. Still, there was no excuse for shooting that poor; didn't even know where the second shot had hit the man!

Extraordinarily bad shooting. Bad enough to get him killed quick in any very bad town up in the American west—though, of course, there were fewer and fewer of those. Place settling down fast, apparently.

Practice was the answer. Hard practice.

Lee had touched the coils of the blacksnake whip strapped to the side of the saddle-bow. Practice with the whip, too.

And what of Juan McGee?

None of the *estancieros* had mentioned McGee after the shooting. Not a word about him. It was difficult for these men to forgive another who hid behind a friend's gun, unfair though that was in McGee's case. The Irishman'd been willing enough to fight; it had been Lee's step in, and Nuñoz' quickness in picking that new quarrel up.

It appeared to take a man his whole life long simply to learn to keep his mouth shut.

A long ride home, that had been—burdened also with considerations of what might be the response of Nuñoz family back in Buenos Aires. Families took odd views sometimes on the shootings of even the blackest sheep. An important family in the Capital . . .

A long ride home, complicated by their coming upon a cow tangled in barbed wire. She'd knocked a quebracha post over, trying for greener pasture, and got her right hind nicely caught in a coil of the German wire. Caught, and torn.

Been a lively time, the three of them quite drunk, to cut her free. And nothing to doctor her with but rum and mud. A lively time.

Three days after that ride, while Lee was with a bunch of his men planting trees down the dirt track to his headquarters (trail had washed out once a week for more than long enough) Sarita McGee came galloping a stocky shewbald, pulled up where Lee was sitting his saddle smoking a cigar, and hit him across the face with her riding whip.

It was funny to hear of that sort of thing happening to other men, usually in the trashier sorts of English novels, of which Lee had several dog-eared and mildewed examples stacked on shelves beside stained cans of horse liniment, hair brushes, tooth powder, saddle soap, American newspapers—some half torn up for latrine paper —jacknives with broken blades, dull razors that needed setting, Barkley's Barley Balm for prickly heat and one of two rat-chewed boxes of Carr's Water Biscuits, which could not be trusted to Bonifacia out in the kitchen.

Funny to read about some cad getting a whipping, usually during a hunting meet, by the proud Miss Lily Whatever.

Not so funny when it happened to you. It hurt considerably, for starters.

Surprised him so much—the first glance directly into that flushed tear-stained face, blue eyes so dark they looked black. "You've murdered my father!" she said, and, while Lee still sat his saddle goggling as the gauchos near them also goggled, she'd clipped him hard across the face with that braided riding whip. And it had hurt like sixty.

The girl had gone on, after Lee had managed to catch her wrist to block a back-swing that looked to be liable to take his head right off, to call Lee a despicable son-of-a-bitch, and a man who, once a friend, had shamed her father past bearing.

If Sarita McGee had had a knife, no doubt she would have drawn it against him as they were, stirrup to stirrup. Failing that, and being unable to hit at him again with the whip, she had spat into his face. The gauchos, shovels and spades forgotten in a litter of seedlings, stared up at them as if they were two-headed freaks hot from the Provincial fair.

"I could have let him be shot," Lee had said—unwisely as it turned out, since the girl had been waiting for just such lame excuse-making.

"It would have been kinder," she said, still trying to twist her wrist free to hit at him again. "It would have been kinder to murder him yourself, you filthy American dog!"

It angered him, that last bit, and for more than one reason.

"Shit," Lee'd said, "you can be certain I won't go to the trouble of saving that whiner's bacon a second time."

Lee had never been struck with a whip—though likely to his discredit, he had used his black-snake on several men. He had, therefore, been surprised at how much a length of braided leather can

128

smart, if laid across a man's face. Now, having said a further piece, he was surprised again by another painful novelty.

Sarita McGee leaned suddenly out of her saddle, her face like a fury's, bent her head, and bit into Lee's upper left arm like a wolf. Went right through the material of the shirt into the meat and muscle.

The pain was by no means the worst of it. It was genuinely frightening—a nasty reminder, he later supposed, of what it might have been like to be eaten by beasts in more savage times.

It hurt like hell, and it scared him. Felt like she was biting a chunk clear out of his flesh . . . felt her teeth grinding deeper . . .

Lee, no gentleman at all, clubbed this seventeen-year-old young lady alongside her head as if she were a drunken brute of a man and weighed in at an eighth of a ton of muscle. He struck her hard as he was able with his free arm and fist once, and then again, but she shook her small head, her long black hair flying free of pins or combs or whatever, and seemed to sink her teeth deeper still, as if to cripple him.

Lee then drew back his fist and hit her again at the side of the head—hit her hard enough to kill her, if he caught her fair (missed that, thank God) and struck her free of him, off her skewbald, and down into the dirt, unconscious and bleeding at the nose.

There had never been, he later thought, so stark and windy a silence among men as existed then for a few moments at the side of that track. He on his horse, the gauchos at the roadside—all astonished, embarrassed, and scared.

Beating Indian woman to death was no great matter in the *Chaco*. Was done all the time, in fact.

Beating a lady to death was something altogether different, particularly if she was not the beater's lady.

Were Sarita McGee dead or dying, the *estancieros* and their men wouldn't care if she'd had a kitchen knife buried in Lee's intestines. Those men would care for nothing except catching Lee wherever they could, trying him securely, and building a large fire to throw him into.

So it was the devil to pay, as sailors said, and no pitch hot. Lee's face smarted like the devil where she had cut at him with her whip across his right cheek, to the corner of his mouth. Left arm felt rather poorly, as well; felt as if she *had* bit a chunk out of it. Shirt sleeve bloody to the elbow.

Lee swung down off the dun and knelt beside the girl. Her horse had bolted when she fell. She lay huddled at the side of the track, looking mighty poorly. Lee touched her shoulder, gently eased her over onto her back. Pale . . . *pale*. Eyes closed . . .

Lee was already considering his chances of getting back to Stirrup . . . fresh horse and a spare animal to lead . . . food, ammunition and full canteen. Paraguay would be the make-for. He'd never make it south, nor east of the Capital, either. Was considering these matters when Sarita McGee moaned and opened her eyes.

"Ah . . . Dios . . ." One of the gauchos expressing the general relief.

Lee was braced for more temper as she woke, and would have welcomed it as a sign she wasn't badly hurt, but as it happened, she came to consciousness like a child, still dazed.

Lee, at the time, was supporting her head carefully, still concerned that she might—or he might—have broken her neck. She came awake slowly, looked 'round her, saw him, and didn't appear furious.

"Easy now," Lee said. "You fell hard."

"I didn't . . ." Fairly rusty croak. "I didn't fall. You hit me!"

Lee had hoped she might have had the whole business knocked out of her.

"I hit you—you're lucky I didn't break your neck!"

"And you are unlucky," she said, tried to sit up, couldn't—then on a second attempt made it. "You who mind other men's business for them . . . who humiliate them . . . who make them appear to be cowards. You will wish you had killed me, you pig!" And with that pleasantry, her nose still trickling blood, got herself to all fours, took a deep breath, and climbed to her feet.

She stood, swaying, looking up at him. "You'll be sorry," she said, and wiped her bloody nose on her sleeve. Lee had heard that phrase before—and from women, many times. On this occasion, he thought he might take it seriously.

One of the gauchos, a boy named Ramon, had caught her horse, and led it up to her. The boy's eyes were wide as a baby's. It was not often a stockman saw a *patron's* daughter take a whip to another great land owner—even less common to see that same girl beaten and knocked off her horse. Events such as these were such as could be told and retold all a man's life, enriched by the killings certain to follow.

Sarita McGee had no easy time climbing onto her horse, but she made it. Her small nose was still bleeding like a boy's who'd had the worst of a schoolyard scramble. Might have seemed funny, on another occasion.

Lee called to her as she reined away.

"Don't make a fool out yourself, Sarita! This does your daddy no good at all." True enough— the silly little bitch was only noising McGee's encounter at Soto's more publicly about.

She sent him, though, only one murderous glance, wiped her nose on her sleeve again (the right side of her face was already darkening to bruise) then spurred her gelding out at a hard gallop back down the track.

Bad doings every which way. And, no question, only the beginning of trouble. Lee could certainly expect to see Juan McGee and maybe his riders, too come to inquire about his daughter's rough treatment. McGee was unlikely to be impressed by a whip cut as sufficient reason for a grown man to strike a lady with his fist, knock her clean out of her saddle. The bite wouldn't be sufficient additional, either.

McGee might not be the man he had been; he

was, however, more than man enough to try to kill the man who had abused his daughter. More than man enough for that.

EIGHT

It was a silent crew that finished planting the *quebracha* seedlings along the track to Stirrup, but no more silent than their *Patron*. No more thoughtful . . .

S'eon had once told him a Chinese saying: "Save a man's life and you are responsible for him and his behavior ever afterward." Never seemed truer than now. He'd stepped in at Soto's , shot Nuñoz to pieces, and now had a shamed McGee (and enraged McGee as well now that Lee had handled his daughter so roughly) to handle in turn.

Hard to see it wouldn't have been better to let Nuñoz kill the Irishman. Likely, though, Sarita would have then ridden to whip him for *not* helping her father in the scrape.

Lee'd owed McGee, was the trouble. Juan and his wife had stood friends to Lee when the other *Chacanos* were looking at him more than slightly cross-eyed, considered him no more than some *Norte Americano* outlaw who'd somehow stolen enough money to set himself up as a land owner.

Hadn't been far off the mark, either.

But McGee—a different man, then—had stood up and sided Lee right down the line. Had sold him land. Strange, how a man might appear strong . . . come to find out it was the fellow's wife had been the strong one.

A cold man, a clever man who cared for nothing but cash, might say that Lee Morgan was approaching the catbird seat. Had been able, with the nicest of public motives (the rescue of a friend) to place several holes in a dangerous rival. And, as a direct consequence, tragic to be sure, had had to kill the pride-damaged friend he'd previously saved. It was the sort of human tangle of violence, chance, and tragic pride that any fierce country held a dozen tales of.

And nothing in it to suggest that Lee could have or would have planned to have done just those killings purely for the profit of it. Juan McGee's land, and no Gaspar Nuñoz to dispute it. Juan McGee's daughter, and no father living to say him nay. The daughter, of course, would say nay long and direly, but the same men who would burn a fellow for mistreating another's lady, would—and some in consideration of their own ex-amples—look the other way if a head strong girl of great property (and no family living) was forcibly shown sense by a man strong enough to do it.

A clever man would say that Lee stood near the catbird seat and only had to face Juan McGee and shoot him down, to plant his backside firmly in that throne of wealth. Forty thousand acres of better land than Lee now held, two thousand acres of that in the best cotton this side of Egypt . . . and more, enough timber to rebuild Chicago, Illinois. A headquarters house twice the size and style of Stirrup's.

That land, with Lee's present, would make him one of the great men of the territory—give him leverage, perhaps to become one of the great men of the whole country . . . a *pampaniero,* perhaps, if he chose to move south. Marriage to a young woman of Society in Buenos Aires . . .

Odder ducks than Lee Morgan had accomplished as much.

Given the opportunity.

The dice, for a hard and clever man, had fallen fair. To make up—to more than make up—for the hoof-and-mouth for all the misfortunes that had cost him Spade Bit . . . had cost him Rifle River. To more than make up for these, after many years trying, Lee had only to shoot a stocky, broken-hearted Irishman who, likely, would be more than half-drunk, and kill him.

McGee, now, would certainly present the opportunity.

So Lee thought and considered the rest of that afternoon. His men were quiet at their work. None of the japing, none of the horse-play the gauchos used to enliven any task. They worked and were silent. Range wars were serious business here in the south, since many riders had brothers, cousins, even fathers riding for other neighboring *Patrons*. It is no light business for a man to level a carbine at his father. These land-war matters made better songs after the fact than joy in the doing.

Lee thought about his possibilities through the day into sunset, was somewhat abstracted by them, so that Fat Nacio, behind his back, gestured and winked to Arturo Cruz at seeing *El Fer* (so nicknamed by the wonderful speed he showed— so like that viper's strike—in drawing his revolver and killing with it) on seeing this formidable *Americano* day-dreaming.

"He is in love with her," Fat Nacio told his wife, Felicia (and a real wife, too, married in a church). "He is mad for her and she for him. It was a passion-bite, a passion-beating!" Here, Nacio had gripped his wife's buttocks, grinning. "As we were, my dear! As I still am when I put my hands upon you!" Felicia, though not altogether agreeing, was too fond of her husband, and too frightened of him, to disagree out loud, and before dinner.

For his part, Lee ate little, but sat, still thoughtful, as Bonifacia, muttering spells against the evil eye, washed out the bite on his left arm with permanganate solution—a disinfectant she regarded as very powerful because of its rich purple color.

"All the spirits of this bite, turn on your tails and enter the mouth of the biter! Surely, Urzalee will burn her eggs inside her belly so they burn out entirely and fall onto the ground! Surely she will eat a turtle with her powerful jaws, and have a turtle child by it! A thing with a shell, and a beak . . ."

And so on, all the time she dabbed and poked at

Lee's wound—not after all, a mortal one. These insult enchantments (which Lee himself used from time to time to charm the gauchos, all superstitious as savages) seemed to lose their charm when directed at Sarita McGee.

"Old woman," Lee said, "I thought you were a Christian."

"I am—but neither am I a fool," old One-eye said, and poked the bite harder with a purple rag. "*Jesu* is a good man, the finest of good spirits. Too fine to be called for the work of the world!" (By which she meant punishment.)

Lee half expected McGee to come riding that evening. His men were apparently half expecting the same, since he saw two of them, the Malintzin brothers, ride out with carbines across their saddle bows to stand watch, cutting across the calf pasture at dusk so that Lee wouldn't see them go. And he wouldn't have, except that he'd come out of his privy just at that time.

Lee was expecting McGee—and perhaps a few of his men. He had decided to kill the Irishman, given a fair opportunity to do so. Had decided this not only on the consideration of the seizing of McGee's land, and likely his daughter—marriage being a matter to be decided later (there was always that slender, lovely possibility now dreaming in some fine convent school in Buenos Aires)—had determined to kill the man for his own good as well. The fellow wanted to die.

Lee had decided this, smiled at it, and accepted a notion of himself, now, that was not comfortable. To be sure, he had killed other men for money. A small robbery in Northern California years before . . . a few men shot at his duty in earning wages from Don Luis. All in all, though, very few men killed directly for gain. Not that bad a fellow, surely.

But, like Bonifacia, also not a fool.

McGee, his *estancia*—also his daughter—were like ripe fruit. A hungry man must be a fool indeed to stand by and wait for another hungry man to come and pick it.

As well. McGee was not liable to leave Lee much choice in the matter. Would be coming to establish his courage again as much as to avenge Sarita's bloody nose.

At full dark, then, and no moon for shooting in any case, Lee, with some odd feeling of relief, had shouted for Corazon, and taken the Indian girl to bed.

At dark-before-dawn, Lee was up and break-fasted—a near miraculous pork steak and eggs, most unusual for Bonifacia, and probably intended as a restorative after the demonic bite—and was soaking in a wash tub of hot water and yellow lye soap, when, in shadowy dawn light, the Indian girl came around the corner of the shack to the back yard with such a look on her face that Lee rose up out of the wash tub as if drawn up by his hair, pulled the Bisley Colt's free of its holster where it hung on the pump handle, and, revolver in hand, walked back around the shack corner the way she had come, ready for truly serious trouble.

Nothing.

An empty yard—except for chickens, except for the jaguar cub still curled in sleep where the children had left it tethered the night before. An empty yard . . . a long grapeless grape arbor to the right, the dirt track winding away south through shrub and tall grass, and now only slightly touched by the first light of the rim of the rising sun.

It would be a hot day for this late in the winter.

Nothing. And if Lee had ever seen quite such a look on an Indian woman's face before, he might have turned back, soaking wet, soapy, with muddy bare feet, to resume his bath.

But he looked again as the morning light slowly seemed to rise from the very ground, and saw smoke tracing a wandering way up into the brightening sky.

A thin, wavering column far away to the south.

Black smoke. Miles away.

It was rising very high before the winds aloft caught at it, twisted it this way and that . . . smeared it away into the colors of the sunrise.

It was at *Finisterra*.

McGee's ranch was burning.

No doubts came to anyone on Stirrup that the Indians had come out of the forest. Not the women, not the hurrying, shouting men obeying Lee's orders as he stood naked in his yard, directing this and that—sending two men to relieve the river patrol (though the river patrol was likely dead already, lying in palmetto scrub, trans-fixed side to side and back to front with Benudo arrows), sending other men galloping north and south to Orellana and Gutierrez, warning them because they might miss the smoke, ordering six men to stand and stay in case Cuchillo swung this way, three remaining men to mount to ride with him. The smoke was the smoke of a burning house, towering, where the smoke of a grass fire would have spread a mile or more across, smearing. Camping fires would have wisped much thinner.

Cuchillo was out.

Lee, Fat Nacio, Armando de Gayana, and a gaucho named Jaramillo rode across the flats west of Sochitl at an easy hand gallop, their rifles across their saddle-bows, their heads up, looking hard through the early morning.

Lee was riding a late-cut lanky dapple grey gelding named *Capitan*—a good strider and stayer, but too quick-tempered for stock work. Arturo had tried to beat the temper out of the horse and Lee had tried to ride it out of him in the pasture stock-pond. Neither measure had succeeded.

They rode as directly as they could for the smoke from *Finisterra*. There'd be no help from the cavalry. Cortez and his lieutenant were in Resistencia, the *Sargento* unlikely to order out a column of cavalry on his own. Too damn far for them to ride in any case—short of a week. All deliberate, the troop positioned to protect the railroad from insurrection, not the *estancieros* from Indians ambitious enough to raid out of the *Mato*.

"What would you have me do?" Cortez, as dashing almost as Gaspar Nuñoz had been, replying to a tirade by Raimundo Paz, editor of the newspaper of Sante Fe. "What would you have me do? Allow bomb-throwing *Socialistas* such as yourself to approach and injure the property of the railroad?" He had shaken his dark, handsome head slowly. "No one would enjoy a campaign against the *Indios* as much as I. Do you doubt I would like being the new Roca? But it will never be, old friend. The *estancieros* must encourage their gauchos to use their rifles on the Benudo men, their pricks on the Benudo women. In this way, civilization, of a sort, will come to the *Chaco*."

Boos from those assembled in the Kit Kat Club.

And so much for the cavalry. Necessary also to give great credit to Cuchillo. It is no simple matter to trot out of a great jungle, wade and swim a dangerous river, then walk and trot some fifteen miles further on past patrolling gauchos to strike at a Chaco *estancia*—the meanest of which, with its armed men, barbed wire, and night guards for the stock, had about it some of the aspects of a fortified camp.

No simple matter, no small matter to plan such a journey, such an attack with simple savages liable to be discouraged and afraid if an owl of the wrong sort flew across their line of march.

Of course, there'd been a late moon. A night too dark for shooting . . . Lee had congratulated himself on that delay in trouble from McGee. Now McGee was very liable to be beyond troubling anyone. Cuchillo, who would be by no means ignorant of the gossip of the *Chaco,* who measured each of his enemies for certain sure, had of course picked McGee's ranch for the very reason of his public indecisions, his sadness, his uncertainty.

Lee was, beyond question, riding the wrong way and had handled his men poorly, as well. The sensible thing to have done would have been to leave a guard at his place, then ridden with all the rest of the gauchos hotfoot to the Paraña. There, with a little luck, they might have caught the Indians crossing back over the river as they had to cross; if Cuchillo were to linger on the grazing side of the Paraña while the gauchos of several ranches gathered against him, he would be a dead man, and his warrior destroyed.

The Redmen would be crossing the river now. They would have made their march by darkness, attacked *Finisterra,* then pulled back to the river in haste.

Lee didn't imagine the attack had been a walkover. If not McGee, then old Cesarpiña would have seen to that. The Benudos would have taken losses . . . and should be crossing the river just about now . . . early morning. The men Lee had sent to check the river patrol might get a shot or two at them, no more.

Cortez would say he'd missed a fine chance to permanently civilize the *Chaco* by rushing off to *Finisterra* (where he could likely do no good) and in so doing, give the Indians a free road and crossing, home to their palaces of green.

Cortez would be right. And for what? For an ageing Irishman . . . a girl with a bloody nose?

The horses had rested enough. Time for some belly-to-ground. Lee whistled and whipped up the grey and his men spurred their horses behind him. The four of them hammered over short grass and long grass, chested through scrub and thorn shrubs flying, the front of their *sombrero* brims pressed up against the crowns by the wind of their passage.

It looked to be becoming a lovely day—"a good day for dying," the Crows used to say along the foothills of the Rockies.

Lee hardly ever let a man gallop a horse hard on Stirrup—the gauchos were bruising riders. There was now, it had to be admitted, a pleasure in riding neck-or-nothing through a lovely morning, plunging through clearings, shallow sloughs in bright sudden sprays of water. Feeling the dapple grey's muscle coil and uncoil beneath him, sense the cushioned jar of the hooves. The wind not yet furnace hot striking light soft, rapid blows at his face. Hear the grunts, the squeak of leather, the clipping rattle and thud of the hooves behind him as the gauchos followed hard.

He had read that the rebel general, Robert Lee, had said to some officer on viewing the Government army approaching his Fredricksburg works in line after line of regiments, bands playing, flags flying, "It is well that war is so terrible else we should become too fond of it."

A wise man.

The grey rushed a ragged hedge of thorn, gathered itself, and sailed up and up and over, for all the world like an English hunter rather than an Argentine stock handler. Lee heard the gauchos shouting, yipping behind him as they tried their horses at the thorn.

A wise man, the rebel general.

An hour later or a little less, they rode abreast and well separated, reins in their teeth and rifles ready in their hands, up the broad raked avenue to headquarters house at *Finisterra*.

A fine, broad, raked avenue lined with young pecan trees along the ditches. Very fine, and leading to what had been a handsome house.

No house there now—only the black and broken structures of a sudden ruin and stinking at every charred timber of fresh fire, burnt paint, melted tin, melted nails and hinges, cracked and discolored glass. The stone pillars the house had stood so high upon, now stuck up through the collapsed wreckage like teeth in a monstrous jaw.

The house had seemed quite large to Lee when he'd visited there. High-ceilinged, airy, ten rooms to it at least. It had shrunk as it had burned.

The left end of the porch still stood, with a patch of flooring. Some freak of the fire and its drafts had saved that remnant, good for nothing. Lee had had breakfasts on that porch when he was staying with the McGees . . . when he first came into the country. Sausage and scrambled eggs, hot sweet rolls and Columbian coffee. Conchata McGee presiding, pouring coffee and cream, black-haired, almost as beautiful as her daughter.

Times gone by. Gone forever, now.

Lee and the Gauchos rode in slowly, walked their horses through thin drifts of smoke, smells of scorched paint, smells of burning meat.

A dog barked . . . barked again.

Lee gestured de Guayana and Jaramillo off to ride around the other side of the run. He and Nacio kept on, reins in their teeth, Winchesters cocked . . . ready.

NINE

They met at the back of the house—and found
Juan McGee there. The Benudos hadn't touched
the Irishman's body, hadn't taken his head,
hadn't peeled his skin. They must have considered
he had some medicine left, after all.

McGee lay out beside the laundry shed, no
clothes on him but a pair of trouser. Must have
heard the Indians, the first of the killings, while he
was in bed. Pulled on his trousers, took a pistol in
his hand, and ran out to fight.

They hadn't touched the weapon, either. A big,
clumsy, English revolver, a Webley or something
of the sort. McGee still had it held in his right
hand.

The Irishman lay just as he'd fallen, a long, fire-
hardened spear driven into his belly. Gunshots to
finish him, it appeared, from the trade shotguns
the Redmen so prized. The Benudos had done
McGee another honor. They'd left a man he'd
killed (likely with that British pistol) to lie beside
him. Where the Irishman's body was huddled in
the last convulsion of death, the Benudo warrior
had been well laid out, his black-painted arms

149

crossed over his belly where Indians thought the soul resided, his iron-bladed knife thrust into the skimpy breech clout the forest Indians favored, his body spinkled with small yellow flower petals, with pinches of yellow flower pollen some shaman must have carried along in a plugged reed tube for the purpose of so honoring any dead.

McGee had done well enough. There were worse ways for a fighting man to lie in death than with an honorable enemy.

There was no sign of Sarita McGee.

Two gauchos lay just beyond the blacksmith's shed half a stone's throw from the back of the house. The Indians had cut these men into pieces —taken one man's arm and placed it at the other man's hacked shoulder . . . had done that, exchanging their body parts and pieces, their heads, until Jaramillo who swore he had known both men well could not tell, weeping, which had been which. There had been no weapons left with these men. The Indians had taken them as they would have taken all other weapons on the place, all but McGee's.

The dog, one of McGee's little fice hunting hounds kept for flushing up bustard and the like, was barking madly at Lee and his riders . . . barking as if he couldn't stop barking. The Benudos had not molested this animal, had left the frantic little dog tied to the chicken coop by its length of cord. Tied there, no doubt, to keep varmints from the chickens.

The Benudos knew dogs very well—would have come upon the *estancia* in deepest dark, and from down-wind. Likely people were already dying when the dogs began to bark.

No sign of Sarita.

Fat Nacio called to Lee from the place where the stable had been burned as the house had been burned and Lee reined the grey over, reining by hand, now, the Winchester resting on his saddle-bow. There were no living Indians in this place.

Lee saw the ruins of the stables. McGee had taken great pride in their extent, their cleanliness. "Cleaner than he keeps the house!" Conchata McGee had said. "I think he comes and throws buckets of mud on my floors when my back is turned."

From the fire-black wreckage of these stables, a sweet, heavy, greasy smoke still leaked, drifted in dark tendrils on the morning breeze. It smelled rich as cooking. Pork cooking.

"*Ah . . . Madre . . .*" Jaramillo was a young man, not much more than a boy, and appeared to have a tender nature as well. The young gaucho dismounted, stared into the ashes, the burned timbers of the stable a moment more, then trotted a few feet away as if on some errand, bent, and vomited into the dirt.

Fat Nacio, irrepressible, winked at Lee. "*Asado,*" he said. *Barbecue.*

Lee swung down from the grey's back, mighty reluctant. Walked over to a place where a cross-beam door had fallen in, clearing a narrow path into the ruins. A few roof planks, burned ragged as black, torn paper, still stretched above this space. The smell was thick as gravy.

The women and children were here.

The Benudos had herded them here, lacking time for more invention—had herded them in, and burned the place.

Lee had never been so foolish nor had any man he'd known who'd known Indians as to believe that they committed such acts wantonly. They never did so, as far as Lee knew, except perhaps when they were drunk. As much could not, in fairness, he said of white men.

Indians made murders such as these for other reasons than simple savagery. These were performances for the gathering of power—power from the spirits of those who died in agony. It was, as the Redmen saw it, that very agony and drove the enemy spirits forth, that enabled the shamans of the Benudos to distill power from them.

Not much different in its way—perhaps not different at all—from the fires and stakes of the Catholic Inquisition. Forgivable, Lee supposed, in time, as most of the world had forgiven the Inquisition.

Perhaps a dozen women, perhaps one or two less than that. More children than a dozen. Several more. And all heaped in a collapsed and twisted pile. They had fallen together, clung to each other, caught fire in their heap. Blazed with fire, roasted and cooked alive . . . screaming . . . screaming . . .

Their flesh had run and melted together, broiled and smoking.

It was difficult to make out each one, to

separate them. More difficult to know them, even by size, by age. Very difficult. It was necessary to walk to another place around the ruin, get a different view. Even then, a man couldn't be certain.

"She is not there, *Patron.*" Fat Nacio. "That one they have taken with them."

It appeared to be so. And if it was, Sarita McGee would soon wish (if she didn't already wish) that she had died with the other women and their children, in their funeral pyre.

Lee mounted his horse again, ordered Jaramillo to mount, and, with the gauchos once more in line abreast with him, rode slow, wide circles over the headquarters property of *Finisterra*.

The dog barked at them as they rode as if to make up, perhaps, for not barking soon enough on a dark night with a late moon.

Lee and the others rode west to the pasture fencing, then swung north. They found most of the *estancia* horses in the high corral. The horses had been hamstrung, each and every one.

It took a while to shoot them all. Lee recognized Sarita's skewbald among those animals. It seemed to take a very great while to shoot all those horses. Fat Nacio had no more jokes to make once all the horses were dead. A very somber fat man he had become.

Finished, Lee and the others rode east and up the arroyo where the *Finisterra* gauchos had their shacks. They found these huts as they had always been. The Benudos had burned nothing here. This arroyo had been the fighting ground, the killing ground. The Benudos had attacked here first to catch the gauchos unprepared. They'd attacked here—sent perhaps half a dozen warriors up to the headquarters house.

"Forty *Indios,*" de Guayana said, leaning low from his saddle. "Perhaps forty-five."

Their horses were skittish, picking their way through the scattered bodies. Gauchos roused in the small hours, perhaps by the scream of some throat-cut man butchered as he slept, had come out with knives, rifles and revolvers. Had been swarmed there in the dark, flooded by rushing, barefoot, black-painted savages. Speared, hacked with trade-axes, *machetes,* war-clubs studded with rail-tie spikes.

"Five or six *Indios,* I think they killed. No more than that," de Guayana. Fat Nacio and Jaramillo had nothing to say. Lee had nothing to say.

The Benudos had taken some time with the dead gauchos. And some perhaps not quite dead. Things had been done to their eyes . . . other parts of them.

Lee and his men rode through the places those dead men lay. The Benudos had left none of the warriors they had lost here. Those dead they had taken with them.

Old Cesarpina lay naked at the head of the arroyo, his knife in his hand—likely had been trying to get up to the house to protect his *Patron,* the *Patron's* daughter. There were blotches of blood in the dirt near the old man's body.

"This old devil didn't die easily," de Guayana

said. "He cost them a man or two, I think." De Guayana dismounted, crossed himself, and stood praying silently moving his lips. Lee and the other two men took their sombreros off, sat their horses 'til de Guayana was finished.

"They took the poor *hija* with them," Fat Nacio said, as they rode back up to the ruins of the house.

"Yes," Lee said, "they took her." He pulled the grey up at the side of the wrecked house where a part of the porch had not been burned. The hound was still barking at them from its tether at the chicken shed.

The four of them sat silent. No noises but the soft creak of saddle leather . . . Jaramillo's black blowing softly through its nostrils.

The morning was already hot, announcing the furnace of full day to come. Lee looked south, and saw the sight he expected to see. High, high in a milky blue morning sky, small circling specks hung swinging in great slow circles through the air. The kites . . . the vultures gathering, turning thier great spirals closer and closer to *Finisterra*.

This place had lost its luck when it lost its lady. Conchata McGee's foolish horse had killed them all. Destroyed them. Though it was possible that Sarita might live another day or two until they were finished with her. Until they had taken their pleasure, and all her power from her.

"Now, listen to me," Lee said to the gauchos. "This is what you will do. You, Nacio and Jaramillo, you will stay here to make what decent arrangement of these people that you can before other men come to help you with the burying. Keep those birds from the dead, do you understand me?"

They did.

"De Guayana, give me your horse." The animal was a big-rumped roan and tired as Lee's grey, but it would do to lead for an extra. "Go and untie that dog; bring him here."

"*Patron,*" Fat Nacio said, "you are never dreaming of going into the *Mato* after them? You will not find her—you will not find their village . . . "

"Be quiet," Lee said, "and get about your business."

The dog, flop-eared, mud-colored, flea-bitten, lay silent in de Guayana's arms as he carried the animal up to Lee. The little hound made no disturbances, either, when Lee hauled him up onto the saddle-blow, holding him there with his right arm.

"Give me the cord." De Guayana handed that up, and Lee coiled it and put it into his jacket pocket.

"If you are going," Fat Nacio said, "then I am going."

"You will do as you are told to do," Lee said, "or I'll notch that other ear for you. Now give me the lead for that roan."

He turned to tie the roan's lead rope to the cantle ring of his saddle and, without saying anything more to them, turned the grey toward *Finisterra's* handsome, wide, raked avenue, and kicked the horse into a trot; the weary roan, farting, trotted after.

"Vaya con Dios," de Guayana called after him. The other two called nothing.

It was a long ride to the river. The horses were exhausted, sweat-lathered, stumbling in the heat. Lee had changed to the roan near a ruined farm that had once belonged to a man named Cruciero. The change made not much difference. The horses were worn out . . . stunned by the heat.

At the river, after they'd drunk, both animals seemed to pick up, to be ready to ride a distance, but Lee knew better. He'd ridden the bottom out of them. Be lucky if they'd take him across the Paraña without rolling to dump him or simply sinking under the drown.

Lee dismounted, knelt in the mud at the river bank to drink a good, full drink, then stood, mounted the grey, and booted him on into the river. Didn't think of the little cannibal fish, either. Had other things on his mind.

The grey drove on in with a heave and a splash, the roan trundling after. The river current, brown, slow, and steady, was not too much for either horse, tired out or no. Lee, once the animals were well swimming, heading out for the center of the stream, slipped off his saddle to the right, to drift there, clinging to his saddle horn, listening to the whimpers of the perched hound crouched trembling at the saddle-bow, its paws awash.

The river swept some of the weariness from Lee —swept some of the edge off the visions he had seen at *Finisterra* as well. The water, though likely warm as soup, still felt cooler than the air . . . a refreshment. At least until he recalled the piranha. The recollection came about midstream, and destroyed much of his pleasure in the coolness of the water.

He waited, after that, for some short quick touches of pain to come flashing, tugging at him, tearing at his legs.

Quite destroyed his pleasure in the swimming.

No piranha came. No disturbance in the muddy current but the regular chug-chug of the horses' legs as they forged ahead, the small hound's whimpers as it lifted first one wet paw then another, huddled high as it could huddle on the soaked saddle.

The opposite bank was steeper and seemed to take a long time to reach. Lee was happy as the horses when they reached that bank, more than happy to be stomping his sopping boots up onto dry land—or the gravelly mud that fairly passed for it.

Here, along this bank, towered the wall of green. It would be no pleasure working down along the river's edge, trying for the place Cuchillo had crossed. Looked to be a serious task just working through the edge of the jungle, even with the river on his right.

Lee tied the horses off to the great bowed root of a wild *tricanda* tree some two hundred feet tall.

They'd be in shade here . . . should be waiting for him.

The hound, relieved as Lee to be out of the river, was sniffing for this and that along the forest's edge—came nicely enough when Lee softly called to him, submitted with only a weak slight struggle when Lee used his bandanna to tie its muzzle shut. Wouldn't hurt its tracking, but if it turned out to be able or willing to track the war-party at all, would keep it from barking.

This small dog, considerably subdued, Lee tethered him to his left wrist by the length of cord, then went back to the horses for the Winchester, an extra box of .44's and his canteen.

Unlikely the Benudo village was more than a mile or two from the river—though from what point of the river, only the little hound might tell him, marking where the Indians had crossed, headed into the *Mato*.

Only a mile or two . . .

Afternoon already. It would be evening by the time the hound found where they'd crossed downstream. It would be night in the jungle. Only late rising moon tonight. Just enough, if he was lucky . . . if he was very lucky. Just enough to see glimmering high through the towering canopy of the great trees. Enough, perhaps, to guide him back to the river.

Lee didn't think of Sarita McGee at all. Hadn't thought of her since he'd ridden from the ruins of *Finisterra* to follow Cuchillo. There was no use thinking of her. No use thinking of the luck that would be needed to find her. No use thinking of the luck that would be needed to bring her out of the jungle.

There was not that much luck in all the world.

Why, then, when there was no use even thinking about it? Perhaps so the girl might not be so hopelessly lost—might not be alone, all alone in the Green Hell to die.

Even here along the edge of the *Mato,* following the high river bank as closely as he could, Lee found the going confoundedly difficult. A trudge and tramp, soaked now with bitter sweat in place of river water, through thick stands of thorns and take-me-too, the sun hammering down at every step that took him clear of shadow, the little hound tugging silent at its cord. All a stumble and a struggle in such enraging heat that Lee would have welcomed the coils of any sort of snake for the pleasure of breaking them.

And this laboring going on and on—more than four miles of work that felt like forty—until, thorn-ripped and worn, near sick with the sun, the clouds of insects buzzing and biting, swarming around him, Lee saw the hound suddenly sprightly, dashing through the thicket to the river, then back again, moaning with excitement through its bandaged muzzle.

Lee went down to the river bank, the dog frisking around him. Saw the marks there, plain. Took no mountain man or scout to know those marks. Prints of bare feet . . . a neat hole in the soft mud here and there where a warrior had used his spear butt to hoist himself up the steep.

They'd crossed here. Gone into the *Mato* here. Gone where he needed to go.

TEN

She had wakened to her father's shouting.

Then shots. Had heard one of the house girls screaming, but not for long.

Sarita had sat up in her night dress, reached for the small nickel-plated revolver in the drawer of the bedside table, then climbed out of the high bed, her heart beating like a bird's, to shouts, gunshots ringing from the arroyo where the gauchos and their families lived.

No more sounds around at the house, though. Up here at the house it was quiet.

She was no coward.

Sarita cocked the pistol, held it steady in both her hands—wished to light her bedside lamp, then decided not to—and walked out of her room into the high-ceilinged corridor, the polished floorboards cool to walk on. The noises echoing from the distance, from behind the corral, behind the stable, were dreadful. Women screaming. More gunshots.

The house was quiet.

She walked down the corridor, past the reflections of the long mirror opposite the entrance to the dining room. The dining room had been her mother's pride. The English table . . . white linen.

Sarita wanted to call out for her father, then decided it was not the thing to do. She was afraid that if she called and he didn't answer, then he was surely dead.

She walked down the corridor into the great parlor. All quiet here . . . quiet here as it was noisy out there in the dark.

She walked across the parlor carpet—French carpet, that had cost the stud fees of his best bull for two years running. Terrible complaints about the price of that during two years of breakfasts, her mother smiling, pouring coffee, paying no heed at all.

The front door was open to a hot night, dark outside as in. No moon at all. Some woman was screaming awfully out back. Sounded worse rising out of the distance, the darkness, like a black fountain of sound.

Sarita said, "Daddy . . . ?" and stepped out through the doorway.

At the first instant, only for the very first instant, she thought the strong hand that gripped her arm was her father's, warning her perhaps to be silent. Reassuring her . . .

Then she smelled the wood-smoke smell of the man—saw, even in darkness, black and glittering eyes.

She turned with the pistol—or tried to turn with it, and was seized at the back of her neck with a grip so savage, so powerful, it was like being bitten there by some great beast. She was held that way, as a puppy or other young animal might have been held and shaken fiercely so that her head flopped this way and that as if her neck was broken.

This Indian, holding her in that way at the back of her neck, reached out with his other hand and took her small revolver from her.

Then, in a rush, muttering something, he shoved her, threw her forward off the porch and down onto the porch steps so that she hurt her wrist trying to reach down to save herself the fall.

"Please," she said, as if she were talking to some rough white man who might understand her and perhaps apologize for being so rough.

The Indian came down the steps behind her, seized the nape of her neck again in that painful, crushing grip, and hauling her back up to her feet, shoved her ahead of him again out of the yard. She staggered under his grip, bent half over, like a child being bullied.

The woman was still screaming. Children were screaming too, but Sarita was sure that she was not. It seemed an awful humiliation to her, to begin screaming. It seemed the worst thing she could do. It seemed that screaming as those women were screaming would turn her into a *thing*. A thing that could never stop making that noise.

The man's grip was hurting her terribly. She had never thought of Indians as strong. Most were small, stocky men, brown and broad-chested. They looked sturdy enough, like good stock horses, but she never thought of them as being so terribly strong—as strong almost as Lee Morgan had been when he'd clubbed her. Sarita'd never been struck by a man. Never struck by any man at all. It had been Conchata who had spanked her when she'd needed it—when she'd plucked poor Roberto, the parrot, quite naked, and put a miniature diaper-cloth on him. When she'd frightened Nana with the devil mask, and caused her to drop a good portion of the Christmas dinner.

Her mother had spanked her. Her father, never.

Now, she thought, now I have been hurt by two men's hands.

The Indian shoved her along before him, pushing her so hard that she nearly fell, then yanking her upright again by that murderous grip at the back of her neck. *I'll be bruised. I'll be black with bruises there . . .* The Indian pushed her forward, shoved her around the corner of the house and into the light.

The back yard . . . the walks . . . her mother's garden. Naked men stood in torchlight, their faces painted black, lips, ears transfixed with quills and feathers. Some carried guns—trade shotguns or taken from the gauchos. Most leaned on long bows, on spears.

The Indian who had Sarita by the neck suddenly threw her down onto her knees and took his hand from her nape. It felt wonderful not to have the pain there.

Sarita saw her father lying on his stomach by the laundry house. At first, in the flickering light, she thought that he was breathing, or weeping as he lay there. Then she saw that it was only the light and shadow that made that seem so. An Indian man was lying near him.

There were woman and children—Sarita thought the Indians had brought them, brought their own families with them. Then she saw they were women and children from the place. One of the women, Eustacia Malinche, stared and stared at Sarita as if she were waiting for Sarita to shout at these savages, to drive them away from *Finisterra*. A child looked at her, too. Several children were looking at her.

They kept watching Sarita as the Benudos began hitting them hard with the butts of their spears, hitting them hard swinging blows with the flats of machetes, with bow-staves, driving them into the stables. *They are going to lock them up. Then they are going to leave them alone . . .* Sarita wished the Indians would put her into the stables with the other women so they could all be together . . . so that she would not be so alone in the firelit dark with the Benudos.

She wished it until she saw what the Indians were doing with their torches, with bundles of lit straw, burning tufts of alfalfa—tucking these small flames into the stable doorway, tossing them into the small windows, tucking them into spaces and cracks in the stable planking.

The women inside made various noises. Some of them shouted in anger at the *Indios*. There was a moan, too, that swept out of the small building from them, a moan like wind in a summer storm— just the sound that wind made at corners and the dormers of roofs.

One of the women threw her baby out of the building, threw it out of the main door, and a young Indian man ran to pick it up, went to the door, and gently handed the screaming child back in.

Horses were neighing in there, smelling the smoke.

A woman crawled out of the left side window and lay down alongside the building in the shifting shadow and light from the flames. Two Benudo men went and lifted her to her feet—they were not rough—and brought her around to the main door of the stable and pushed her in.

As soon as they turned away, however, this same woman (who Sarita thought was named Emmanuela, a sister of the woman married to Porfirio Gomez) crawled out of the smoke from the doorway, crawled as quickly as a naughty child determined to escape a bath.

An older Benudo came up to the woman, frowning, as she crawled across the yard quite quickly, he caught up to her and began to strike at her head with a hard wood club. When he hit her the first two times, she continued to crawl. But when he hit her a third time, she stopped crawling and sat down in the yard and put her arms up to try to protect herself. The Indian hit her again, though, and her arm fell down. Then he hit her in the head very hard, and Sarita heard the crack of the woman's skull as it broke.

The woman still seemed to be alive, though, because she sat in the yard for awhile and didn't fall over, though she shook her head from side to side like a horse troubled with flies.

Then, when the fire blossomed up and the stable began to glow with the brightest possible light—when the women inside, as though in a sort of appreciation, commenced sounds . . . howls . . . one of the same young Indians who had pushed her back into the stable to begin with, came over to the head-shaking woman and pushed the point of his spear into her back.

Sarita crouched in the dirt of the yard, in just the sort of fire light she had enjoyed countless times at *asados,* campfire parties . . .

She and the Benudos watched and listened together to the thundering light, to the extraordinary noises the women and children and horses made as they were burning.

An old Indian with a wide mouth and slanted black eyes, turned to look at her once, when the sounds became almost too shrill to hear, shrugged, and smiled apologetically, as if the whole affair was proving uncomfortably noisy.

It all took a surprising length of time, and during it, Sarita lay down in the dirt, curled on her side, and began to pretend that other things were happening than were happening, and in another place than this.

Later, when *Finisterra* was quiet again, nothing sounding through the darkness but birdcalls, some murmured conversation among the Benudos, final soft seethings from the fires, a man came to

Sarita, bent down, and bound her hands together behind her back with cord. He tied hard knots.

Then he kicked her—his bare feet hard as pony's hooves—until she staggered to her feet.

The Benudos, murmuring, were filing out of the yard, trotting out to the back pasture. The Indian who had bound Sarita now took her by the hair and dragged her into line with them and pushed her on her way. She walked, wincing, barefoot, as if she were one of them, walking through the dark behind a short Indian who smelled like a clean dog, walking in front of the man who had bound her hands behind her back.

When she slowed or stumbled, this man behind her shoved her hard, so that she was afraid she would fall against the Indian walking before.

Her feet were hurting on thorns . . . stones. The Benudos had stopped talking with each other. Now they made no sounds at all. They walked very fast as if they were about to begin running. There was a dog barking back where the house had been . . . the stables. The dog was barking as if it would never stop.

It was a cool morning, but there was that slight smell of iron in the air that predicted a very hot day.

Once over the pasture and a mile into the scrub, Sarita's feet, which felt as if she were walking on splinters of broken glass, began to slip from under her in the oddest way so that twice she tripped and fell, scratching her arms, tearing her nightgown on thorns and briars.

These two times when she fell, the warrior behind her reached down and jerked her to her feet as easily as she might have, when a child, picked up her doll, Mercedes. The Indian did not hit her, didn't say anything to her at those times. He remained as silent as the others that filed away into the darkness at their pace of near-running, going as certainly as if they walked an even road by daylight instead of a wilderness by night.

Sarita often had to run to keep up. She was afraid that the Indian behind her would hit her as the other Benudo had hit the crawling woman back at *Finisterra*. Her feet felt very odd, though. She thought perhaps they all were walking through some rubbish pile the gauchos had created throwing garbage, animal bones, broken bottles and all sorts of broken glassware and rusted barbed wire, all that pointed, sharp-edged trash out here where her father might not see it and order them to clean it away.

Walking on those sorts of things would explain why her feet felt so painful . . . so odd.

She fell again, rather to her surprise, since she'd thought she was doing well keeping up with the others. But she slipped, and her feet felt like wood, and she fell.

The warrior walking behind her picked her up again and said something to someone else. He shook her hard so that Sarita's teeth clicked, then suddenly lifted her right up in the air—her whole body. He swung her up into the air like a bundle so that the skirt of her gown flew up over her knees like a white ghost in the darkness. He heaved her up and slung her across his shoulder like a sack of feed, and not so heavy a sack of feed at that.

Held her up there, hanging head down like a fool, and set off walking after his fellows as though he was carrying nothing at all.

At first—jouncing rythmically along across the Benudo's shoulder, the man's right shoulder hard as wood under her belly, the man's right arm hard as wood across the small of her back to hold her there—Sarita thought that she might become ill. Might vomit. The thought of this happening frightened her so that she forgot about becoming ill and vomiting and after a while, went to sleep.

She woke weeping in moonlight, her head aching fiercely, all the brush she was seeing rocking slowly upside down as she was carried along over the Indian's shoulder, her head hanging down his back. It felt like being carried by a horse. There was the same sort of patient strength under her but much more uncomfortable this way then sitting up riding. The grass brushed her long hair as the man walked along, still walking that swift, almost trotting walk.

Sarita didn't fall asleep again. She dreamed, though, with her eyes open, watching the grass stems combing through her hair as they traveled along. The blood pounded softly in her head at every stride the Indian took. She supposed that she might die just from hanging upside down . . . She couldn't feel her legs at all, though she knew she should be ashamed for the Benudos to be seeing her bare feet, her ankles and calves. She supposed that if she couldn't feel them, the matter could not be too serious.

ELEVEN

They reached the Paraña at dawn, and when the
Benudo, not too roughly, set her down into the
grass at the river's bank, Sarita thanked him, even
though sitting upright made her feel ill for a few
minutes. She would have thanked anyone who had
set her down onto the grass.

The Indians waited at the river bank only long
enough for the last of their line to gather, and that
was hardly any time at all. Then an old man with a
wide mouth whose face she remembered said
something that made some of the other Benudos
laugh, then snapped his fingers like a man
summoning a waiter in Buenos Aires, and
gestured the men nearest it into the river.

These jumped straight in and commenced
swimming as neatly as frogs out into the muddy
current. It was a pretty morning, the sun just
edging the horizon. Sarita started to think what
might become of her—a secret she was certain
most of these Indians knew (the old man with the
wide mouth must know it)—then decided to think
of other things. She hoped for a moment that
piranhas might attack the Indians swimming

175

across, then decided not to think of that either.

No unpleasant thing was worth thinking about.

She sat in the grass, watching the Indian men jump into the river and start swimming. They swam with the alacrity of animals and sometimes turned, laughing, to dash spray at the men swimming with them.

Children, Sarita thought. Like most men. And thought it so unfair that such children—men—should have that power. Should have the strength in their arms, the careless energy and anger to injure gentler people.

The sun was almost up, the heat from it driving with its light, striking at a slant. Two of the Benudo men came to Sarita and although she tried to stand up to show that she would go into the water, would swim, they paid no attention. They took her by her arms, pulled her to the river bank, and swung her once, then threw her out into the river.

Cool, cool brown dark—ease . . . ease for her injured feet; she had looked at them, sitting in the grass, the soles cut, stiff with dried blood.

Now, though, the river came swirling all around her, soaked her and bathed her . . . pressed her gently down. It occurred to her that here was a safety the Benudos could not breach. All that was necessary was to open her mouth to the river and let it in.

If she had been older—had lived as a woman, if only for a little while—she might have been able to do it.

She came to the surface and a young Indian

near her in the river dashed a spray of water at her, laughing. He was a handsome young man, for an Indian, with eyes as bright as jet, teeth white as sugar.

Sarita smiled at him, and the young man, delighted, smiled back, and splashed her again, but more gently. He said something to her in Indian, then started swimming out across the river, smiling, beckoning her to follow him. One of the Benudos on the near bank shouted to the young man, and when the young man shouted back, laughed.

It was a long swim across the river, and Sarita grew very tired. She swam slower and slower until she didn't swim at all. She thought the young man might come back to help her, but he didn't. Another man, an older man with a white eye, swam up beside her, doubled up his fist and hit her in the face. Then he took her arm and pulled her after him, swimming. She didn't know why he had hit her.

At the other bank, so steep, they had to carry her up to the *Mato*. There, they tied her hands behind her again and the man with the white eye put her up onto his shoulder and carried her into the green.

All that day they left her in peace. Left her in a hammock to rest, to sleep as she chose. The hammock was swung from the posts of a large open palm-thatched marquee—a public place near the edge of the village, a place where the women came to cook, where children played, gathering from time to time to watch Sarita as she slept, or rested with her eyes closed.

Whenever she opened her eyes showing their dark blue, the children would scatter like flushed birds in terror. The women paid no attention to her, awake or asleep. They stayed by the open pit fires, talking, dozing in their own hammocks while the meals—whole monkeys, skinned, some pots of chewed root—cooked over smoky fires.

Men walked through this place; they never stayed.

The day passed in the slow advance of shadows across the village clearing. There, Sarita could see the men talking around their own small fires, playing with their children, and sometimes standing to shout and do a sort of dance, brandishing whatever weapon they held—recounting, Sarita supposed, their bravery, the victories in the fighting at *Finisterra*. None of these Benudo men did any work during the whole day as far as Sarita could tell, except that one shaved slight strips from what might become a bow-stave. The task took him several hours and seemed no nearer completion at the end of that time than at the beginning.

Sarita lay in her hammock, trying to keep her bare legs covered with the torn fabric of her nightgown which was now dirty as a kitchen rag. Once, one of the women, quite a pretty girl with beautiful hair and a pleasant face only spoiled by her tattooing, came over to Sarita with broad leaves, dark green as jade, on which she'd placed some small bananas, a mound of mashed root, and a small piece of meat stuck on a stick. Sarita smiled and thanked her, and the girl turned away and did not approach her again.

Sarita ate the bananas—a thing the children came near to watch her do—and she tried to eat some of the mashed root (she felt she would need her strength to run away in the night, which she intended to try to do). She thought she might well be able to find her way out of the *Mato,* find her way to the river. The Benudos, seeming so inhumanly complete in their ferocity the night before, now with broad daylight, had dwindled slightly into naked savages. The man she was sure was *jefe,* the redoubtable Cuchillo, had resolved himself into a bony-chested old man with a mouth wide as a monkey's. He had been the one who'd shrugged and smiled at her while the stable was burning.

Sarita tried some of the mashed root which tasted like torn wet cloth, and not something to eat at all. But she did not try the meat; its odor made her feel sick.

Shortly after she'd eaten the bananas, Sarita was seized with a violent necessity of nature, sharp cramps that caught at her, made her afraid she would lose control of her bowels. This troubled her more than the thought of running away into the *Mato* at night. It was an immediate and dreadful humiliation.

She had seen some of the women wander off into the undergrowth beside this cooking place and she had seen the children doing their business where they pleased, like dogs, trotting away to leave their mess behind them in plain view.

She lay for a while longer trying to control herself, then could not wait any longer. She called to the women around the cooking fire, asked them whether it was permissable to be excused. None of the women appeared to understand her, none appeared to know any Spanish at all. They sat at their fire and stared at her like dumb things, not like human women at all.

It was impossible for her to wait. Impossible.

Sarita got out of her hammock, and, as the women watched her, walked as slowly as he could from under the shadow of the thatch out to a growth of long-leaved brush just at the jungle's edge. She thought for a moment of running then, even in daylight, but the cramps seized her too strongly, and she bent, crept into the foliage as well as she could, crouched, tugged her nightdress up, and relieved herself, the filth making noises as it left her in a rush. Shame, and unspeakable relief.

She looked up, still crouching, and saw, past the droop of leaves, two Benudo men standing watching her from the cook-shed. They stood leaning on their long spears, watching what she was doing—must have walked over to watch, when she left her hammock.

Sarita bent her head so that her long hair covered her eyes. They could see her but in this fashion, she could not see them, so her shame was less.

There would be no running away into the forest in daylight.

By evening, more of the men were dancing. They danced at their small fires just as the gaucho's children danced when they were pretending to be Indians, in their play.

The Benudo men sang sometimes as they danced. Nothing much to hear, as their dancing was nothing much to see—a shuffle this way, then that. Some finger-curling gestures as if to mark more clearly what they were singing about. Some of them were smoking tobacco, puffing at it in long wooden pipes, blowing clouds of smoke. The women didn't go across the clearing to join these singers and dancers.

The trees, encircling the village, so towering high, shaded out the setting sun as cliffs might have done, and the village sank into darkness as if into a sea, the fires growing brighter, the faces of the savages around them glowing red—painted and tattooed, quilled and feathered—against curtains of dark.

The drumming—wooden clubs on wooden sounding boards—the nasal droning of reed pipes, the Benudos' repetative chanting, all served to make Sarita sleepy, to lull her, to allow her some ease.

She had been thinking that her father's friends would believe her dead with the others in the fires. Lee Morgan . . . a brute . . . would surely think her dead. A brute and a fool, to have shamed Juan McGee.

A man may be a fine-looking man and still be only a fool. Americans had the reputation of being foolish people, and now she had seen it. Poor Gaspar, who had been so handsome. Shot to pieces, the gaucho women had said. Shot to pieces. . .

Sarita started to think of her father, then tried to think of something else—of other things, than horseback rides with her father when she was a little girl. How he would come, early in the morning, to wake her, sushing Nana, who slept in a bed against the wall, saying "Shhh . . . no need to wake the Señora . . ." and then dressing Sarita himself while Nana watched, wondering at the ways of *Patrons* with their children—how they adored them, and treated them like jewelry. And particularly so in the *Chaco,* where most little children, however coddled, died.

The *mestizo* women could not understand such attachment to a creature so manifestly frail, so almost certain to fail and be buried. When the child grew older, of course, that was a another matter. A strong, growing child—say of about eight years—that was a great treasure, if a boy.

Her father would dress Sarita like a lady in her own riding habit cut in miniature by the finest tailor in Resistencia. It had been blue and was very warm to ride in, though it set off her eyes. Her mother had said the material set off her eyes.

Dressed, ready, her little whip in her hand, she had tiptoed down the corridor behind her father—

down the corridor, across the parlor, and out to the porch and the waiting horses.

Those morning rides . . . those morning rides. The dawn flooding the skies for her in new colors every time. The world made new for her, new in odor, in color. The world made new each morning. Memories so much more real than this, this crouching half-naked and dirty in a rough-woven hammock. Listening to the savages drumming . . . singing their peculiar songs.

Coming back from the rides, her mother would be waiting on the porch, sitting at the breakfast table while Eleanora brought in the platters of eggs and pork steaks and sweet rolls and fried banana. "Ah," her mother would say, "my two gypsies have returned to me . . ."

An Indian man came into the thatched shelter, stood by Sarita, and looked at her. He was a young man with braided scars deliberately made as decoration running down both his arms. He had a broad and brutal face, but he didn't look at Sarita in a threatening way. It was an interested look, almost friendly.

Sarita wondered if this man might speak Spanish. She had thought that if one of the Benudos could speak Spanish—and would speak with her—she could tell them that her father . . . that *someone* would be willing to pay a great price if she were allowed to leave their village, escorted safely over the Paraña. If they would do that, then Lee Morgan or Señor Orellana would be more than willing to pay what they asked. Axes . . . or shotguns. Perhaps even a repeating rifle for the old man with the mouth like a monkey's.

"Habla espanol?"

The broad-faced young man appeared interested in her speaking, but he didn't seem to understand what she'd said. Which might mean that he didn't speak Spanish, or might mean that he didn't choose to speak Spanish now.

Two other men—these very young men, boys younger than she was—came across the clearing and stood beside the broad-faced one, looking at her.

Then, two old men came, one the one she was certain was the *jefe,* Cuchillo, with his wide mouth and slanted eyes, the other an even older man. These two went and squatted at the nearest cook fire (the women left it, and went to another). The second old man commenced to make odd noises in his throat, coughing, and hawking, and spitting loudly as if he were ill. While he squatted making these sounds, the old man also began to gesture, making signs and motions with his hands. Then he took a little wad of leaf from a small bag at his waist, stuck out his tongue, and put the wad of leaf on it. Began to chew it.

Another man came and squatted near Sarita's hammock. He was picking his teeth with a sharpened twig and had a wound on his side—a knife-cut, or a bullet graze—plastered with chewed green leaves and red mud. He was an unpleasant man and gave Sarita an ugly look.

"Habla espanol?"

The men seemed interested to watch her talking, to listen to her. None of them said anything in reply, although one of the young boys (both quite naked) said something to the other boy that made him laugh.

The old man by the fire commenced to sing, stopping from time to time to loudly clear his throat and spit into the fire. There was foam gathered on his lips.

Sarita turned to look for the women. They were sitting by the back fires, playing with their children, throwing fresh river driftwood into the fires so that bright clouds of sparks fountained up into the darkness.

TWELVE

Now, with night, the jungle was coming alive.
Chirps, grunts, shrill trilling calls sounded from
the dark. All those noises sounded very close.

The broad-faced man leaned over and put his
hand on Sarita's arm just below the sleeve of her
nightgown. He and she both looked there, where
he was gripping her—his hand, wide-palmed,
stub-fingered, scarred and deep red-brown, in odd
contrast to her slender upper arm, so very white.

"Let me go," she said, as she'd said it to
Manuel de Torrejon several years before when
he'd tried to bully her as they played together.

The broad-faced man paid no attention to what
she'd said. He rubbed her skin with his thumb, the
hard callous scratching her, as if to see if her
whiteness might rub away.

"Let me go," she said, and tried to pull her arm
away. She looked back to the women, but they
were talking, paying no attention.

Cuchillo still sat at the near fire; he was talking
to the other old man, who was quiet and sitting
still now, spittle running down his chin.

One of the very young boys, his eyes as bright

187

and black as jet beads, reached out and touched
Sarita's bare right foot. She drew her foot up
under the torn skirt of her nightgown, but the boy
reached under there and gripped her ankle.

"Damn you!" Sarita said to the boy—she was
afraid to speak like that to the broad-faced man
who held her arm.

She kicked out and the boy jumped back a little
and took his hand away from her ankle. One of
the men who was watching laughed.

"Go away!" Sarita said to them. She was afraid
to look at the man who held her arm. She was
afraid he might drag her out of the hammock and
push her into the fire. She was afraid he would do
something.

For a little while, the Benudos stood silent,
watching her, the palm oil on their faces glistening
in the firelight. The old man by the nearest fire,
the man sitting with Cuchillo, was making clicking
sounds with his tongue against the roof of his
mouth. It was the loudest noise anyone was
making.

The broad-faced man moved a step or two, up
to the head of her hammock, but he didn't let go
of her arm. Sarita remembered the Indain
breaking the crawling woman's skull.

She felt sick to her stomach; she felt that she
would vomit if they didn't go away from her.

"Go away . . ." she said, and the boy who had
done it before reached up under the hem of her
gown and took her ankle. She tried to kick but he
held her too hard.

His friend, the other boy he had been laughing

with, leaned over and put his hands on her other foot. When she tried to pull her foot away, the boy hit her leg with his fist. He did it so suddenly and it hurt so much that she screamed, just for an instant.

When she did that, the Indians immediately seemed to become relaxed and pleased. They laughed, some of them, and made signs and said things in their language.

The broad-faced man, standing behind her head, said something to someone, then let go of Sarita's arm and reached down to take both her wrists, one in each hand—and suddenly pulled them up and back so that her arms were held up and back over her head.

Half-lying, half-sitting up in the hammock, Sarita suddenly convulsed with terror, thrashed and tried to pull her arms back down, tried to kick out, to make them let her go.

The Benudos became very friendly when she did that, and smiled at her, and nodded in a pleased way. One of the men who was watching came to her side and smiled down at her and said something to her in Indian.

"Please . . ." Sarita said to this man. "Please."

The unpleasant man with the plastered wound on her side got up and pushed in beside the man who'd spoken to her.

Sarita turned her head awkwardly, because of the way her arms were being held above her head, and saw that the *jefe,* Cuchillo, was not watching. He was talking to the other man.

The first boy who had put his hand on her ankle

held her ankle with one hand for a moment. With his other hand, he pushed the material of Sarita's gown up her legs and when she bucked, trying to kick at him (her eyes wide as a frightened horse's) the unpleasant looking man reached down to tug at the material, tore the gown a little, and pulled it up over her hips. Pulled it up higher so that she was naked from her belly down.

Sarita screamed then and doubled up to hide herself, and kicked out as hard as she could, harder than she ever tried to do anything. She turned her head to try to bite at the broad-faced man's hand but he tugged her arms out straight over her head so that she couldn't reach him.

She tried to pretend then, that she was dreaming, that the men weren't looking at her, that they were all blind and couldn't see where she had hair in her secret place.

She bucked up and down like a pony, then tried to draw her knees up to conceal herself, but the two boys wouldn't let go of her legs, they just wouldn't let go though she began to beg them and beg them, babbling like a baby, her voice rising higher and higher while the Benudo men, very pleased, watched and listened to her, open-mouthed. The boys especially, as they clung to her ankles, as they held her despite the most desperate struggle she could make, gasping with the effort of it. The two boys seemed very excited, very proud of holding her so hard, of not letting her legs loose for an instant.

The hammock swung a little this way and that as she fought, but the boys each had their grips and kept them.

When she began to scream again, one of the men (the man who had spoken to her) leaned over her and struck her in the mouth with his fist.

This broke her lip, and blood ran down her chin.

Sarita was afraid to scream any more, though that had given her great relief. Now she was afraid to do it.

She lay panting silent for a few moments, and the Indians were quiet, too. Sarita felt her heart pounding so hard it was making her sick. It would serve them right if she was sick on them . . .

I can't help it if I'm naked, she thought. It's not my fault if they can see. Elsa Fuentes had once showed her thing to Sarita when Sarita was staying with her in Sante Fe. It had had a little patch of blond hair on it. She had asked to see Sarita's, said all the girls in the convent showed their things to each other, but Sarita hadn't let her see, thinking herself ugly, with so much black hair there.

If they want to see how ugly it is, Sarita thought, I can't prevent it.

She was sweating from the heat of the night and the heat of the fires. She was weeping, too, though she didn't remember starting to cry.

The boys tugged at her legs, slowly spread them wide apart to either side of the hammock. They pulled her legs so far apart they hurt her.

One of the men said something, and he and another Indian bent over her. She felt them put their hands on her thighs, and she tried to twist away, to pull her legs free.

One of the men laughed and put his hand on her, right there where she was hairy.

It was the oddest thing—Sarita heard howling, and knew it was she making the noise. But she couldn't stop; it was the oddest thing.

She lay, half-sitting in the hammock, her nightgown pulled up to her breasts, her legs held spraddled wide, her head thrown back as she screamed . . . howled . . . like an animal.

The Indian put his finger up into her.

He pushed hard with that, pushed hard and hurt her so much that she became sick, and gagged and vomited a little sour vomit. It ran down her chin. She struggled to pull her arms down. She felt that if she could pull her arms down she would be all right. It would make a wonderful difference . . .

Out of breath, choking on a mouthful of vomit, she lay gasping for breath. They were all looking at her down there, watching what the man was doing with his finger, watching him hurt her there. Some vomit was caught in Sarita's throat and she coughed. She couldn't breathe well—it was something to do with the way the broad-faced man was holding her arms back above her head. If he would let her go, she'd be all right.

The other man was pinching her down there, hurting her. She felt him pulling her thing more open. He was hurting her all the time.

The boys were hurting her, too. They were pushing on her legs so her knees doubled, so they could hold her feet higher, spread her legs wider apart.

The man pulled his finger out of her, and then

held it up in front of her face so she could see it. It was red with blood.

A man pushed this man aside and stood beside the hammock staring into her eyes. He was doing something below his waist, and Sarita saw that he was naked, and his thing was stiff and swollen, sticking straight out. He was rubbing it while she watched. Some of the other men laughed.

Then he stopped that, bent down over the hammock and felt her where she was naked, down in there. She felt his hand on her behind, and when she tried to turn, to twist away from him, the two boys pushed her legs higher up, further apart, so that this man could touch her anywhere.

He touched her behind, and felt her there, and then put his fingertip where her dirt came out. He pushed his finger in there, and hurt Sarita so badly she couldn't help screaming again, but not so much screaming as calling out.

"Help me, please . . . ! Oh . . . oh, somebody please help meee . . . !"

She shrieked out as if God Almighty were up above her, high, high in the great trees, and would float down like a huge condor, with wings as dark as the night, to save her and bear her up.

The man took his finger out of her behind. Then, as if he were in a great hurry, he swung his left leg up over the hammock and straddled it, reached out to grip Sarita's naked hips with both his hands, lifted her, hunched himself forward in the webbing, and poked at her where the other man had hurt her, where the hair grew.

The Benudo was going to do to her what the

bulls did, the stallions she had seen in pasture, mounting the trembling mares, driving their huge organs into the mares. The thing the gaucho children giggled about behind the cotton shed. Doing the thing that had made her mother cry out in the night, cry as if she were being terribly hurt.

"No, no . . ." Nana had said to her, when as a little girl she had wept and confided that Papa was hurting her Mama in the night. "No, no," Nana said. "It is a love they are making," and had slid her forefinger through her other forefinger and thumb circled. Slid it back and forth. "That is what they do—making the love. Your Mama likes it—that is why she cried out when it is done to her."

It was something Sarita, as a child, had half believed and half not.

The Indian, squatting close up between her splayed knees, reached down to adjust himself while the other men laughed and talked among themselves, watching what he was doing.

Then he pushed his thing into her and it was much bigger than his finger had been, and went up inside Sarita until she ached with it.

She grunted as he pushed it into her—and she called out for her mother, and then grunted again when he pulled his thing almost out of her down there, then shoved it in again. It made a sound going up into her. It hurt her.

Sarita turned her head away so as not to see the Benudo's dark, sweat-polished face as he strove against her, doing a thing so *close,* doing the closest thing that could be done to her. When she turned her head, she saw that some women standing off behind the men had come from their cooking fires to watch. They were watching what the man was doing to her. Children were there, too, giggling and then covering their mouths.

The ache was up into Sarita's stomach from what the man was doing to her. *Fucking* her. The gaucho children used to tell her they watched their parents doing this. Called it *fucking*.

He was fucking her.

A small boy crawled to the other side of the hammock. Sat down there, glanced up at Sarita, looked into her eyes, then looked away, stared up through the hammock mesh at where the man was doing it to her.

The Benudo's face began to change. He jolted into Sarita harder and harder, bruising her, hurting her inside. She felt her small breasts tremble as he struck into her, the nipples feeling strange as they rubbed and rubbed against the cloth of her gown. Her insides hurt, and also felt strange . . . felt as though a thing within her was moving, starting to turn over inside her. It was a strange, forboding feeling—as if, if he kept on doing what he was doing, the Indian man would break something, change something so much that she would die.

The Indian's face looked odd, distracted, as if in the midst of doing this thing to her, he had thought of something else entirely, some thought that had seized all his attention while he moved faster and faster against her, thrusting, beating against her down there, jolting her in the hammock so that the sweat flew from her.

The man made a whining sound in his throat—held still for a long moment there between her spread knees. His eyes were closed, squeezed tight shut, and Sarita felt him shake between her legs, felt his thing inside her move with a slight, slow, steady beat.

The pain inside was slowly soothed, became almost something pleasurable, a sort of ache that nearly was a pleasure. It was very strange.

The man stayed crouched that way against her, and took deep breaths. Sarita heard the watching women murmur. She had the oddest feeling, listening to the sounds the Indian women made as the man, warm as an animal, still pressed hard against her—she had the oddest feeling that she would like to open herself up like a book to show them all her insides. All her secrets. Would like to pull her gown up higher so that the Indians could see her breasts, see how her nipples had been rubbed and made hard by the cloth from what he had done to her.

She thought there was more inside her than they could bear to see.

When the man pulled suddenly out of her, it hurt her badly. She started to cry out, then closed her mouth on the cry so they wouldn't hear it.

Her thighs were aching very badly. They were hurting as badly as cramped muscle hurt. She thought she would begin to yell if they didn't let her close her legs, let her move. She strained, tried to move her legs, but the two boys holding them held hard.

The man sighed, lifted his left leg over the hammock, put both feet on the ground and stood up. His thing looked much smaller than it had. It was wet with something, and blood.

Sarita lay back as well as she could. She tried to ease the muscles of her back. She was running sweat, and something, some moisture, was oozing from her, drops of it trickling from her thing down her behind. The two young boys were looking at her there as they held her legs wide. They were staring at that place. One of them took one of his hands from her ankle, and reached down and touched himself. His thing was stiff, but not as big as the man's had been.

One of the Indian women came through the crowd of men, walking through them to the hammock. Several of the men's things were exposed, swollen and stiff, thrusting out from their hips. The woman, who was an older woman who had been pretty, came to the side of the hammock and looked down at Sarita. She looked into her face, then reached down to pull her gown up to her shoulders, and looked at Sarita's breasts. Then she reached down and felt Sarita's thing, tugged gently at the wet hair there. The woman put her whole hand on Sarita and squeezed her there gently.

The unpleasant looking man suddenly pushed this woman aside and, as the other man had done, quickly straddled the hammock, freeing his swollen organ as he did.

"Please . . ." Sarita said to him. He stared down at her where she was so open, reached down to grip himself—and stopped what he was doing as the other men stopped laughing.

There had been a sharp noise—something. Sarita thought that someone, one of the gauchos perhaps, had dropped a plank where they were working in the saw pit. It was such a relief . . . such a relief to be waking from a dream so shameful she would thank the Virgin on Sunday for waking her from it.

That same flat, sharp, ringing sound. Just behind her, a man grunted as if he'd been struck. Sarita grasped awake, woke from no dream, and turned on her side very easily, her legs free, the man gone from between them—to see the broad-faced Benudo lying against the hammock post behind her, blood spraying in a wonderfully bright fountain from his throat. Bright, bright crimson in the firelight.

Beyond him, as she craned her neck to see through the hammock's meshes, the wide-mouthed old man, Cuchillo, had fallen forward into his small fire. His face was buried in the coals, and his short black hair, only streaked with gray, was burning.

The Indians shouted and were dancing back, watching their war-chief burn in his small fire. The man sitting opposite him, who had coughed and spat and chewed the leaves, jumped up as Sarita watched him, jumped again and fell back down as the third shot sounded. Lay stretched and quivering.

The Indians walked backwards, away from these fallen, their hands over their mouths. Sarita tried to sit up, to climb out of the hammock, but she couldn't; she couldn't move to do all that. She heard footsteps, running. More of those fine, sharp, ringing sounds, more of those gunshots.

Lee Morgan came into the firelight with a devil's face, raised his rifle as Sarita watched, and shot down a Benudo half across the clearing as the man began to draw his bow.

Then, moving faster than she could quite follow, he whirled to break his rifle against a roof post, turned back drawing his revolver, and firing two shots with it into the crowd of Benudos, knocked two men down and kicking.

Then he came to her, lifted her up out of the hammock, and walked slowly backwards into the shelter of the forest and its night, firing slow, measured, aimed shots as he went.

The Benudos were not creatures to be long afraid of anything, not even the death of their *jefe,* not even the death of their shaman.

As Lee carried Sarita with him back into darkness, back into whispering leaves, curtains of veins that stroked them on their way, back into darkness deeper than darkness, there came a swift buzzing, hissing, humming flight of spears and arrows seething through the woods like rain.

After a considerable time, she was able to walk, half supported on Lee's arm, the little hound trotting beside.

They walked on a soft, damp cushion of rot that glowed here and there in small patches as they passed, fields of spoiling fungus shining dully as their footsteps made it tremble.

They walked, the girl wearing Lee's jacket over her torn gown, through a cathedral of trees taller than any church that man had built—great pillars, half lit here and there by faint beams of moonlight shafting down from the murmurous canopy that roofed this church of moonlit black and green. These trees, these titans grew a pistol shot and more apart, huge, columner, ribbed with surface running roots standing higher than a man, that snaked away like great monsters' tails into the dark.

Things moved beneath their feet as Lee, the dog, and Sarita McGee made their way by indefinite late moonlight toward the wide, slow river running to the south. Small things, and some things larger moved away—scuttled, coiled, or scurried to the side.

The girl had clung to Lee at their first rest, had hugged him and wept. She'd said nothing to him, however, and he'd said nothing to her. She had petted the little dog, though, and seemed glad to see it.

She was light to carry and they would have made better time in that way, after the moon was up, but it troubled her to be carried; she began to struggle weakly to be put down, to be allowed to walk, much like a kitten tired of being fondled.

So Lee let her walk. And after the first little while, she walked well enough, though she limped. They walked in silence. Lee going first, she following, through the mazy patchwork of light moonlight and shadow, lighter dark and pitch. Once they heard the Indians calling to each other, a distance away. And another time, later, they heard a man clicking his tongue against the roof of his mouth. The little hound had whimpered softly through the bandana bandaging his muzzle.

They had heard a man make that clicking sound —and then heard nothing more.

Sometimes, as they rested for the girl's sake, sitting above the rotting forest floor on one of the huge, sinuous roots, the jungle would slowly come alive around them, its creatures booming, whistling, calling through the darkness.

Sometimes this terrific noise continued as they walked on, and sometimes it didn't.

These silences, Lee thought, might betray them, though they seemed haphazard, whether Lee, the girl, and the dog were moving or not. To the Benudos, however, these matters might not seem haphazard at all . . .

Lee had the Colt's reloaded and didn't regret the Winchester. Better to break it than leave it whole to the Indians—and he couldn't have carried it with the girl. The girl. She stunk of Indian . . . had the starchy smell of jissom about her and limped badly.

They'd been screwing her when the little dog, tracking, led Lee to the village edge. A buck mounting her as Lee knelt to get a bead. It was a shame. A gently bred girl—even an *estanciero's* daughter raised in the *Chaco*—would be damaged by that raping, perhaps beyond the possibility of ease or comfort for it.

A shame. Saved at least from the using all the men intended for her. They would have lined and fucked her like a barrel-house whore. Then, if her insides had not been broken to bleed her to death, the women would have been at her with sharp-ended sticks glowing from their cooking fires. She would have given the tribe considerable good luck, good medicine, before she died.

Still—a shame.

They came pretty close to the river, Lee thought, to a marshly place where the girl had great difficulty in walking. Though she tried to resist him, Lee picked her up and carried her a way, the little dog frisking around them in the moonlight so that Lee nearly tripped over him.

Out of this rough patch, Lee set Sarita down, and stood listening. The little hound whimpered, its head cocked. It was the river, Lee thought. There was a sound ahead—slow, soft, various and constant together, the whispering a river makes as it runs a slow descent.

A man clicked his tongue against the roof of his mouth—and not a dozen yards away.

Lee drew as fast as he had ever drawn the Bisley Colt's, shot to the sound, and in the blast and flare of gunpowder heard a man gasp as the bullet struck him. And from another direction, a sharp short hissing.

From where that sound had come, a man now broke out from the brush and came running toward them. A stocky warrior running out of dark into moonlight, his bow-stave in one hand, a trade-knife in the other.

Lee shot him once to hold him still—a second time to knock him down. Then, and still at a distance, he fired a third and blew out the fellow's brains.

No more sound. The forest silent following the noise. No more sound. Lee stood listening, the Bisley cocked, seeming as it always did as such times to be waiting with him as a friend might wait.

Nothing. No sound.

Then, slowly, very slowly, the jungle began its uproar, sounds commencing to echo from the distant canopy until the whole world of darkness took them up.

Lee turned and saw the little hound, tail wagging, trotting over to see how Sarita did.

She did badly.

The Benudo's arrow had taken her under her left arm, and driven into her deep. She knelt in a dapple of moonlight and shade, rocking slowly forward and back, the arrow fletching white in the pit of her arm.

The little dog was much upset.

Lee knelt beside her, the Bisley holstered, and heard the muffled soundings of her blood, loosed inside her, rushing into broken lungs.

"Ah, sweetheart," Lee said to her. "My dear . . ." And held her in his arms.

"*Too late,*" the girl whispered to him, "*Too late . . .*"

And said nothing more.